Ruby Parker Hits the Small Time

Rowan Coleman

HarperTempest
An Imprint of HarperCollins*Publishers*

HarperTempest is an imprint of HarperCollins Publishers.

Ruby Parker Hits the Small Time
Copyright © 2005 by Rowan Coleman
All rights reserved. Printed in the United States of America.
www.harperteen.com
Library of Congress Cataloging-in-Publication Data is available.
ISBN-13: 978-0-06-077628-2 (trade bdg.)—ISBN-10: 0-06-
077628-5 (trade bdg.)
ISBN-13: 978-0-06-077630-5 (lib. bdg.)—ISBN-10: 0-06-
077630-7 (lib. bdg.)
Typography by Andrea Vandergrift
1 2 3 4 5 6 7 8 9 10
❖
First U.S. Edition
Originally published in Great Britain by
HarperCollins Children's Books, 2005.

For Lily

Ruby Parker Hits the Small Time

Chapter One

You can't stop things from changing, because other people—adults—think they always know what's for the best. It's like it's sort of not officially your life until you're grown up. As if the way you think and feel doesn't really matter, doesn't really mean *anything*—almost as if you don't even really feel it. As if, because you are only thirteen, everything you think and feel is just in your imagination. I feel like I should have some say about what happens to me in my life, but I never do. My life just happens *to* me, and other people make the decisions. The wrong decisions, mostly.

Just recently, I've felt like I spend my life trying to keep things exactly the same as they've always been and it's like I'm running up a down escalator. Just when I feel like I'm getting somewhere, I lose my footing and off I go—down and down—until I find the energy to start going uphill all over again. Some of the things that have happened in my life have been amazing. Some of them have been the sort of things that other girls my age lie in bed at night and dream about having happen to them. But I bet none of them dreams about what happened to me this morning. It's like a fairy tale in reverse, with the happy ending at the beginning.

This morning I found out that I am officially the frumpiest thirteen-year-old in the entire history of the world. You might say, like my mum does, that everyone feels that way sometimes, that it's a phase and I'll get over it and one day I'll turn into a swan and boys will follow me around begging *me* to look at *them*. But it doesn't feel like a phase; it feels like the end of the world. The end of *my* world, at least.

If I was just Ruby Parker, girl, it wouldn't matter so much. OK, I'd be doomed to a life of never having a boyfriend, but I could work on being interesting and funny instead, and maybe be "unusually attractive" like the heroines of my mum's books that I'm secretly reading. Once I got past about, say, thirty-five, I expect I wouldn't even mind that much anymore.

But I'm not Ruby Parker, girl.

I'm Ruby Parker, Television Star. And, in my world, being an ugly, dumpy thirteen-year-old means the end of that, and the end of going to my school, and maybe the end of everything else I've been trying to hold together too.

If you saw me, Ruby Parker, standing outside the classroom waiting to go in for math on the last day of term, you'd have said I'm a pretty ordinary girl. Not the sort of girl who'd be singled out for any special attention, good or bad. Sort of medium height, sort of medium build (apart from the obvious, but more about those later), and sort of medium hair—hair that had been shiny and blonde when I was little but has gradually become browner and darker and danker and lanker. I also have average skin (not too many spots), quite a nice nose, and not a bad profile.

You'd notice that most of the other girls in my class really don't bother talking to me, although they frequently talk *about* me, usually in stage whispers behind my back to make sure I can hear everything they're saying. And you'd notice that while I just hang around in the corridor waiting for Miss Greenstreet to arrive, some of the other girls are practicing their ballet positions against the wall, and Menakshi Shah is reciting Juliet's balcony speech from *Romeo and Juliet*, flicking her hair all around as she does it, trying to catch Michael Henderson's eye. (Not that he'd look at her in six million years, because everyone knows that he and Anne-Marie Chance will *never* split up and will be together forever and end up presenting a daytime talk show like *Richard and Judy*.)

Anyway, you'd have noticed that none of the boys talk to me either, although they sometimes creep up behind me and twang my bra strap and say things like, "Oy, Ruby, have you seen my football? Me and Mac lost our footballs and . . . oh, look, they're down your top! Give 'em back!" And they pretend to lunge at me and try to grab my boobs, then I scream and hit them over the head with my folder, and my best friend, Nydia Assimin, charges at them, which usually sends them packing, but still they shout really nasty stuff like, "Watch out, it's a herd of elephants!"

You'd also notice that almost all the boys are pretty well turned out for thirteen-year-olds. None of them smell, and most of them wash their hair more than twice a week. Some, like Danny Harvey (who always smells of apples), wash it every day. And you'd notice that they're all what my mum calls "natural extroverts." You might think that boys are always shouting and mucking around, but the boys at my school do it with excellent projection and perfect enunciation.

That's because I go to a stage school. I go to Sylvia Lighthouse's Academy for the Performing Arts. Every single one of the kids who was standing outside my classroom waiting to go in for math on the last day of the term wants to be an actor, a singer, or a TV presenter—or all three, usually.

We have all our normal lessons in the morning, and then after lunch we have dance, acting, and music until four o'clock, which might sound like a laugh—and it is—but it's hard too. Especially when your speech and drama coach is a raving lunatic, hung up about the fact that she never made it big and ended up teaching a load of snotty stuck-up posh kids instead (which might be why she hates me more than anyone else on account of my being on the telly). But even though I don't have that many friends, at least I have Nydia. And although it can feel like I'm always working and never have time to just relax, I love the school.

School is the only place where I feel like I am actually me—the person I feel like inside and not the person everyone else sees, I mean. When I'm dancing or acting or singing, it doesn't matter that I'm not popular or very thin or that I don't have a boyfriend. And although the teachers make you work twice as hard as other schoolkids, and they remind you that not everyone will make it, they do believe that sometimes dreams come true. I don't know many adults who do that.

I've been going to the academy since I was eight, but it was only when Nydia arrived last year that I made a real friend for the first time. Nydia is quite an unusual girl. She's got the loudest voice in our year and the loudest laugh you've ever heard, which she says is because she always has to shout to be heard over her four brothers, but I think she's just got inbuilt "theatrical projection." Nydia's family originally came from Nigeria, but Nydia was born in the same hospital as me, only two months later than I was. So, like we say, apart from the fact that she's black and I'm white, and the fact that we have different parents and everything, we could practically be twins. It feels like we *are* twins sometimes, because sometimes we just start thinking the same thing at the same time, like a joke or something, and we start laughing for no reason. Then everyone looks at us blankly, but *we* both know why we're laughing, and it makes us laugh even more. It makes me feel safe and sort of warm inside to have a friend like Nydia. While everything keeps changing, Nydia and I will always be the same.

Everyone else here is super-rich, with parents who

are frequently featured in *Hello!* But Nydia and I come from the same sort of background with the same sort of terraced house and normal mum and dad. I'm only here because I got famous by mistake (which pays fairly well, as it turns out). Not that I see a penny. I have a trust fund where most of my money goes until I'm twenty-one. Twenty-one! That's practically my whole life so far again before I get to see any of it! And even though I think I have quite a lot of money, we have a very normal life. Mum says it's important that I keep my feet on the ground so I don't get into drugs and alcohol like some child stars. So I still have to ask her for stuff and she mostly still says no.

Nydia, however, won her place at the academy, beating more than four thousand other applicants through the Sylvia Lighthouse scholarship program, which makes her better than probably anyone else in our year. But that doesn't stop the other girls from picking on her and calling her fat and stupid. Anne-Marie even said no wonder so many people are starving in Africa, because obviously Nydia ate all the food. But she said that in front of Miss Greenstreet and then we got lectured for over an hour about the Third World debt, so she hasn't made *that* crack twice. And she's a moron anyway, because Nydia grew up in Hackney just like I did, and has never even been to Africa. But that's Anne-Marie for you; she has the brains of a pile of damp pants.

Nydia wants to be a character actress, which Anne-Marie says means an ugly, fat actress. But if you ask me, it's better than being a character*less* actress like Anne-Marie, because she looks just the same as everyone else: tall, thin, and blonde, which means she's bound to get a part on *Hollyoaks* (when the current cast gets too old and ugly and gets sacked). But at least they *will* be old, like twenty-five or something. Not only thirteen, like me.

The thing that happened to me that other girls just dream about? I got famous.

Not just a little bit famous like Anne-Marie, whose dad is a film producer and who was once in a Euro-Disney ad on TV.

Not just famous because my dad used to be a rock star and my mum was a supermodel, like Jade Caruso's parents.

Not famous for modeling in the Kay's Autumn/Winter catalogue like Danny Harvey. (He looked nice, by the way, even if he didn't exactly smile. According to Menakshi—who obviously fancies him, as she fancies more or less *all* boys—he thinks he's too good for everyone else at the academy, even the popular kids. She's probably right. He used to be quite a laugh; then about a year ago he seemed to change overnight.)

Anyway, I am famous in my own right. I'm famous because every year since I was six, I've appeared in Britain's most popular serialized soap, *Kensington Heights*. Unless you come from outer space or something, you'll have heard of it. It's set in the cut-and-thrust world of an auction house and it's all about very rich, glamorous people buying antiques (and having sex with each other's husbands, usually). Every year from mid-August to February, *Kensington Heights* runs at eight o'clock on Wednesdays, and I'm in nearly every episode, playing Angel MacFarley.

That's how I got to be famous—and not just in Britain, either. I'm famous in Eastern Europe, Pakistan, and Japan, and even a bit famous in America. I don't know this for sure, but *Kensington Heights* runs on the BBC America channel, and I read in *Heat* magazine the week before last that Brad Pitt watches it and he's a big fan! Imagine that! Brad Pitt has seen *me* on TV! Which is why it's a shame that Angel MacFarley is about as glamorous as a pair of cheap sneakers. But it's only to be expected, of course, because *I'm* not even *slightly* glamorous. Even last year when I went to the British Soap Awards, all the other girls from the show wore backless and strapless dresses and glitter and heels. I had on my black suit and a blue velvet top and no real makeup, just foundation and lip gloss. Mum said I had to look my age. I told her, "I don't want to look my age, I hate my age!" And she said that the only way to get around that was to grow up, which I clearly wasn't ready to do if I was going to make a fuss about it. Like I said, she's pretty keen on me being normal—even when being normal makes me look stupid.

Everyone else in the soap is super gorgeous, of course—except my family, the MacFarleys, because we're what the producers call "social realism." (However, Angel's mum—played by former model Brett Summers—is still pretty attractive, even in a frumpy top.) And, anyhow, I don't know how realistic it was when it turned out that Angel's dad had a long-lost identical twin brother who came back while he was away nursing his sick mother and tried to trick Angel's mum into going to bed with him when normally she'd never cheat, because we are the only family in the soap that doesn't do stuff like that.

In the end, Angel found out about it and stopped him just in time. I got a lot of letters after that episode. You'd be amazed how many kids actually do find out that one of their parents is cheating on the other one (although only two letters concerned actual identical twins). And they get all stressed and upset, and don't know if they should say anything and it's all horrible. I don't know why they write to me as if I actually know anything about *anything* in real life, but I always write back and put in some leaflets and the number for ChildLine and suggest they talk to a teacher if they are worried. The other teenagers on the show get letters from people telling them how much they love them, especially Justin de Souza (who I'm madly in love with, by the way). All I get is people's problems and that practically says it all, to be honest.

Mum says it's because I'm famous that the other girls at school aren't that nice to me. She says it's because every summer break when I go off to film the next series of *Kensington Heights* they wish it was them instead. And I say, "Why would a load of thin, pretty girls, who actually get a holiday all summer long, be jealous of me stuck at the BBC studios filming *Kensington Heights*?" And she rolls her eyes and tells me that I don't know how lucky I am. I suppose she's right, because most of the letters I get from other girls tell me more or less the same thing, even if sometimes they don't always realize that Ruby Parker and Angel

MacFarley are two different people.

The thing is, you don't know how lucky you really are until it looks like everything you have is going to be taken away. I thought it was all right that I was just normal-looking, because my character was normal-looking.

I couldn't have been more wrong.

19 Othello Road
Shakespeare Estate
Birmingham

Dear Angel,

I hope you don't mind me writing to you. I expect you get people writing to you all of the time. I read a bit about you in Girl Talk mag and you said that when the show's on you get nearly two hundred letters a week! Do you read them all yourself or do you have a helper to do it?

I just wanted to write and tell you that you are exactly like me. We could be sisters! My dad's not the live-in caretaker of a posh antique shop, but that's not what I mean. I mean that you and me are exactly the same. I'm always overhearing people talking about things I shouldn't and I'm often getting into trouble for saying the wrong thing. Also I have the same duvet cover that you do. Also my mum drinks a lot too just like yours. Sometimes she gets so drunk she falls flat on her face and everyone looks embarrassed. Sometimes it's not even when there's a party. Sometimes it's in the afternoon. I wish I had a dad like yours to sort her out (my dad says he has washed his hands of her) and of course having a rich uncle to pay for a rehabilitation center must be a help.

I like watching you on TV because you are so much like me and when you get fed up sometimes because Caspian Nightingale doesn't know you love him, you always seem to come through OK. I like you much better than any of the other teenagers on Kensington Heights. You are the only one who looks real.

Thank you.

Love,
Amy Bertram

P.S. Don't worry about writing back. I bet you are busy. Unless you want to, that is.

Dear Amy,

Thank you for your letter. I am glad that you enjoy the show so much and that you identify with Angel's character; she is lots of fun to play. I do get a lot of letters, but I haven't had so many recently as we have been off-air for a while. I started shooting the new season as soon as school broke up for summer a couple of weeks ago, so no holiday for me! The show starts again next week. I think you've been watching reruns on UK Gold, as the story line you describe was two seasons ago. Angel has a different duvet cover now.

You asked me if I have a helper to answer all my letters. I do—it's my mum—and sometimes my cat, Everest. (Although he's not really much help as he sits on the papers.)

I don't know if you saw the helplines advertised at the ends of those episodes about Angel's mum drinking a lot. But just in case you didn't, I've enclosed some leaflets with the numbers on them, in case you wanted to talk to someone about it.

Otherwise you could speak to a teacher if you are worried. As you know, Angel didn't tell her dad about her mum's secret drinking for ages and it really got to her. After she talked to an adult she felt much better about it.

Keep watching the show!

Best wishes,
Ruby x

Chapter Two

*L*ike I said, it was an accident in the first place that I got famous. I wasn't even trying. I didn't have to queue up for six hours with thousands of other girls and then go through six weeks of elimination rounds. I didn't even know I was auditioning. But then I was only six so it's not that surprising, because when you're six you don't really think ahead all that much, do you? When I was six, everyone said I was beautiful with my blonde curly hair and dimples. I even played Goldilocks in the school play, and the Virgin Mary in the Nativity. It's a bit of a shock to wake up one morning and discover that if I auditioned for the same plays today, I'd probably get the part of the fat grizzly bear—or maybe a goat.

Anyway, I didn't go to a stage school back then. I just went to an ordinary school, and then on weekends I went to a drama club, which Mum said I should go to because I was always putting on shows in the living room and doing ballet and singing. Dad agreed I should go if it would shut me up for five minutes. And they laughed about it for ages because they knew he didn't really mean it. He used to love it when I sang to him, even though back then I went out of tune a lot and mostly forgot the right words. They still have all my shows on video, even the really bad ones. Actually, one of them appeared on last Christmas' edition of *Before They Were Famous*. It was the one when I was doing a sailor dance all on my own at the drama club's annual show, and I sneezed and all this snot shot out and ran down my chin. Dad thought it was hilarious, but Mum and I didn't speak to him for the rest of Christmas. I was mortified. I knew then I'd never get a boyfriend— especially not Justin de Souza, who is so handsome that it hurts to look at him. But it was pointless staying angry at Dad. If I had, no one would have been talking to any- one, and what kind of Christmas is that?

So, I'd been going to the club for a while, and then one day Mum made a big fuss about what I was going to wear, and she spent ages doing my hair. And these two men showed up to class and they didn't look anything special to me, except that one of them made Mrs. Buttle, our teacher, go all high-pitched and red. (I didn't know then that he was the famous actor Martin Henshaw, who used to be on a cop show before I was even born, and who's now Angel MacFarley's dad, Graham MacFarley.)

Mrs. Buttle told us we were playing a game and we all had to take turns talking about our mums and dads. Well, I stood in the middle of the room when it was my turn, and I told them how my mum likes to dance to eighties music when she's vacuuming, that sometimes we do the conga around the house for no special reason, and that my dad snores so loudly he makes the alarm clock on the bedroom shelf vibrate. That's all I said. Next thing I knew, I'd got the part as Angel MacFarley in *Kensington Heights*. But I was only six, and, to be honest, I didn't really have a clue what it meant except that I'd go and play "pretend" somewhere other than Mrs. Buttle's drama club and under the dining room table.

I do remember that my mum and dad argued about it for ages, though. I remember that because it was the first really loud argument I'd ever heard them have, even if they were laughing as well as shouting. I remember they went into the kitchen and shut the door as if it would keep me from hearing them. It didn't then and it never has since—not even with the volume of the TV turned up and my bedroom door shut too.

My mum said what an amazing opportunity it was for me, and my dad said there'd be plenty of time for opportunities when I was older. My mum said that there might not be, and that sometimes opportunities don't come twice and she never got any chances when she was my age and she wasn't having me deprived of them like she was. Then Dad asked Mum if she was happy. She said of course she was, she just wanted me to be happy too. And he said that if I had a Barbie and a king-sized bar of Dairy Milk I'd be over the moon, and she said, *You know what I mean, Frank!* And in the end he gave in, because he always did back then.

He doesn't even really have to give in anymore. Mum sort of stopped asking him his opinion recently, which I suppose means that at least they argue less. It used to be when they argued that they'd sort of laugh at the same time, and that later on they'd be all cuddly and soppy. But then—I don't really remember when I first noticed—the arguments got louder and there wasn't any laughing. Or any cuddling. And when they'd finished, after everything had gone quiet, and maybe one of them had gone out and slammed the front door, either Mum or Dad would find me and ruffle my hair and ask me if I was OK. And I always said yes, as if I'd never heard them.

Nydia thinks that Mum and Dad are having a "difficult patch," like a couple we saw on *Trisha.* I hope so. I think as long as I stay out of the way, turn up the TV, and keep saying I'm OK, everything will stay the same and we'll *be* OK. Except everything is changing and it feels like there's nothing I can do. I can see what's happening to Mum and Dad; I can feel it, but I can't seem to stop it. I keep running up those escalators, but I'm still not getting anywhere.

Anyway, as I said, I was blonde when I six and sort of cute and chubby with dimples. Now, according to Amy from Birmingham, I'm the most real-looking teenager on the show. And according to Liz Hornby, who I accidentally overheard talking about me during a script meeting on the set this morning, I'm going through a "difficult lumpy stage." I suppose what she meant is that ever since we finished series seven I've got these two extra bits: the Breasts.

You'd think there'd be a sort of adjustment period, wouldn't you? There should be a warning for when they were coming up. I thought that I was bound to be one of those girls who had to wait for years to get any at all, and that they'd be small ones like Mum's. I didn't think I'd be the first girl in my year to get them. And I didn't think they'd start out being a C-cup! Everyone says that I'm a freak and, by the sound of what Liz Hornby was saying earlier today, they're right. I *am* a freak. A big, lumpy, difficult-stage freak. Anne-Marie is *so* going to love this when it gets out.

You see, the thing at school is that I try to be the girl who doesn't care what anyone thinks. I try to be the sort of witty and sparky girl who doesn't need to be accepted to be happy, who just shrugs off the snubs and teasing and stuff like that. And most of the time it works. OK, so only Nydia laughs at my jokes and everyone else couldn't care less if I was witty and sparky so long as their nail varnish and lip gloss match, but it's a way of knowing how to be.

But then this thing happened and, before I knew it, I'm all pulled out of shape, like I've been shoved back into the wrong-sized box or something. Like, no matter how hard I try to fit it, I never will. It's hard to explain, but once the future seemed like forever away and suddenly it's here. The beginning of being grown up is here and it's nothing like I imagined it would be. (Admittedly, I imagined it would be Justin de Souza pulling up to school on my sixteenth birthday and asking me to go to the Oscars with him, but still . . .) It hurts and it's awkward—and not just because my bra pinches and rubs my shoulders.

Nydia tried to cheer me up about the Breasts when they appeared last term. She said I should be proud of what God has given me, and pleased that I was becoming a woman, and that maybe Justin would suddenly see me differently and chuck his girlfriend and ask me out. And I tried to be pleased—I really did—and I tried to stop hunching my shoulders up.

But then, that day at lunch, Mackenzie Gooding asked me if I had to go through doorways sideways now that I was such a wide load, and Nydia went right up to him and said *in front of everyone*: "I don't know why you're going on about it, Mackenzie Gooding! I bet your willy's so big you have to fold it up just to get it in your pants!"

And all the boys nearly wet themselves from laughing, and all the girls tutted and looked disgusted—especially Anne-Marie. I had to grab Nydia by the arm and drag her into the girls' loos, because nobody could be any redder than I was just then. I said to her, "Nice try, but I think you sort of missed the point a bit."

Nydia apologized and promised the next time she picked on Mackenzie Gooding she'd go on about his *little* willy instead, but I suggested she just forget it. Really, you'd think I'd be used to humiliation by now.

I've had enough practice.

And anyway, I'm sure it's because of the Breasts that I heard what I heard today. I'm sure it's mainly because of them—and a bit because my hair always looks greasy and my skin always looks shiny—that the producers are going to axe me from the show!

Oh, yes, and because I'm ugly.

KENSINGTON HEIGHTS
SERIES EIGHT, EPISODE EIGHT
"REVELATIONS"
WRITTEN BY: *TRUDY SIMMONS*

SCENE SIXTEEN

INT. AUCTION HOUSE: EARLY EVENING

CASPIAN and JULIA lean against a late-Victorian dresser in each other's arms.

CASPIAN
It doesn't matter what they think, Julia. They can't stop us. I'm fifteen now and you will be too in a few months.

I love you, and if you're ready, then,
so am I.

                    JULIA

Oh, Caspian, I don't know. I just don't
know. What would Mummy say if she found
out . . . ?

The door opens. ANGEL comes in looking
for a book she has left behind.

                    ANGEL

What are you two up to? You'd better
not be doing anything in here. If Dad
finds out, he'll go ballistic. You know
that Uncle Henry says he'll ground you
for good if he catches you with her
again!

                    JULIA

Oh, please don't tell anyone, Angel.
Please. They don't know what they're
doing, keeping us apart. We love each
other, don't we, Caspian?

CASPIAN looks a bit uncertain, but he
holds JULIA even tighter.

                    CASPIAN
Yes, yes we do. You won't tell anyone,
will you, Angel?

ANGEL shakes her head. CASPIAN and JULIA
exit, leaving ANGEL looking forlorn and
sad. It is clear that ANGEL has a crush
on CASPIAN and would do anything for
him.

Chapter Three

Anyway, this is how it happened. I didn't have much to do on the set today—no crying or anything hard. Just Angel finding out that her cousin Caspian, who she's in love with, and her father's archrival's daughter Julia are still seeing each other—despite being totally forbidden to do so by both of their parents. Also, Caspian is trying to get Julia to have sex with him, but she's not sure she wants to. She probably won't in the end though because *Kensington Heights* in no way condones under-age sex; we leave that sort of thing up to *EastEnders*. Or possibly she will say yes, but they'll get found out and stopped in the nick of time—probably by Angel. Angel's main thing is finding out stuff and stopping it in the nick of time.

So, I didn't have much to do, but I couldn't go home because I had to do some reaction shots at the end of the day. That's when you look just off-camera and have to pretend you're reacting to a line another actor has said. Sometimes the actor's not even there! Sometimes it's just one of the runners or something, saying it all deadpan like they're ordering a Big Mac and fries and you have to gasp or cry or something. I used to be terrible at reaction shots; I always wanted to laugh instead. But then Liz, our producer, would say time is money. So I'd put a tear stick under my eye and think about what it would be like if Everest ever died, and usually it turned out all right in the end.

Brett and Martin had this big scene to do, and Brett said I was putting her off just hanging around watching and that I should go for a walk or something, so I thought I'd go and see Liz because she's really nice normally. I knew that Liz was upstairs in some kind of emergency script meeting, and because one day I want to write my own screenplay with Nydia (we've already started writing one) and direct my own film (an independent one with Justin in it because we'd be married by then), I thought they'd let me sit in on the meeting. They have before.

I got there and the door was open a bit, and so I

thought I'd just wait for a lull in the conversation before going in, but then I heard my name! I heard Liz talking about *me*, Ruby. So I thought, *Excellent—new story lines!* I crept up a bit closer and put my ear next to the crack in the doorway, and that's when I found out.

"It's just that Ruby seems to be going through a bit of a . . . a difficult stage right now," Liz said sort of sadly.

"Yes, she is a bit. She's just sort of stuck between being a girl and being a woman. She does look a bit awkward, poor thing," Simon Jenkins, the script editor (who I now know to be evil), said.

"I don't think it's that big of a deal," said Trudy, the show's main writer. "She's just a normal girl. She gets loads of fan mail from girls just like her. She appeals to her demographic. I know that *KH* is partially about glamour, but not everyone can be glamorous all the time, and I thought we wanted a balance. Otherwise we'll end up like *Crossroads*, and look what happened to that! It's not as if she's the star of the show. I think we should let her grow a bit and then decide."

At first it felt sort of strange listening to them talk about me, like they were talking about some other girl. Like it wasn't about me at all.

"I agree with you up to a point, Trudy," Simon said.

"But, say what you like, it *does* matter what people look like on TV. The public likes looking at pretty faces. It *is* important and, well, if you-know-who is worried about it, then we have to be too. That's just the way it is: for a lot of people out there, she *is* the show."

I heard Trudy sigh and someone shuffled some papers. It felt like a dream, like one of those nightmares when you walk into class in your knickers and nothing else and everyone laughs and you think it's real. And just for a second when you wake up you feel sick and terrible. Except this wasn't a dream. And I wasn't going to wake up. I wanted to run away, but I couldn't. I was sort of glued there.

"So," Liz said after a pause, "what are our options?"

"Well," Trudy said crossly, "bearing in mind that we're talking about a child here, we have a few options. Option one: We send Angel away to America or something and she comes back as a different actress—a more photogenic one."

I felt my stomach turn over and my mouth go dry. And there was a wave of panic in my tummy just like when a roller coaster starts going down really fast.

"Option two," Trudy continued, "and my favorite—a bit of a cliché, but always a hit—we give Angel a makeover. Maybe put a few highlights in her hair, get her some colored contacts, and let her wear a bit of lip gloss."

I remembered wearing lip gloss at the British Soap Awards and feeling like I had raspberry pudding glued to my lips. Yet before I could get used to the idea, Simon chimed in: "But do you think Ruby's got anything to work with? I'm not sure a makeover will cut it."

There was a short silence and it was like I was watching a live link on satellite telly—like there was a two-second delay between him talking and me hearing what he was saying.

"Option three is that we kill her," Trudy said.

Bang. Just like that. My knees went weak and I had to grab on to the wall to stop myself from falling off the world. It was just like someone really had told me I was going to die. In that second it all caught up with me and I realized that if I went from the show, everything else that was just about holding things together in my life would go too.

I'd never get to see Justin again, which meant he'd never get to know me properly and realize one day that it was me he loved and not his stupid girlfriend. And, worst of all, Mum and Dad would be so disappointed in me, so angry with me that they might stop trying altogether, and then . . .

And then I had to stop thinking about it. I had to stop before I started crying and they heard me or something.

"Oh, yes," Simon said. "I like that option. Let's kill

her. She could have some sort of disease. We could tie it in with National Kids Dying Week or something like that."

Trudy moaned. "Oh, Simon, you are such a—" I think Trudy was going to swear, but Liz stepped in before she could.

"Ruby is such a great little actress," Liz interrupted. "I know she'd give that story line everything, but, well . . ."

I couldn't listen to any more after that because suddenly I felt sick. My head was throbbing and my cheeks were burning. I ran out of the building and onto the lot and tried to get as far away from everyone as I could. I ran into one of the Portaloos and locked the door. My face was all hot and I felt like I should cry, but my eyes were dry and prickly. I get letters from girls who are picked on at school because they're fat, because they wear glasses, or sometimes just because they're different. And I write back to them and say I know how they feel, because everyone feels isolated sometimes and it's best to be true to yourself and talk to a parent or teacher. But I *didn't* know. It wasn't until then that I knew how they felt—so alone in the world that there was nothing they could do to fit in, because it wasn't anything they *did* that was wrong. It was everything they *were*.

It took me ages to be able to go back to the set and

act like everything was fine. Actually it took until one of the runners came and banged on the door and shouted my name. A part of me wanted to just walk out of there and leave them in the lurch. But I'm not very good at rebelling, so I just went back and I did my scene. Luckily I was filming reaction shots for a scene when Angel accidentally finds a robber in her house and I had to scream and look scared. It was pretty easy. After all, it's not every day that you find you're going to get killed, is it?

Flat 32
Mandela Tower
Freedom Estate
Luton
Beds

Dear Ruby,

I hope you don't mind me writing to you. I'm sorry to be taking up your time. It's funny though, because I'm thirteen like you, and I feel like you know me really and that talking to you is like talking to a friend.

The thing is, Ruby, I don't know what to do at the moment. I really don't. My best friend, Becky, stopped talking to me a couple of weeks ago. She got in with the in-crowd and then just stopped talking to me. And it wasn't just her—it was everyone. Nobody talks to me anymore. It's not like anyone calls me names or hits me or anything, but all day long at school, I'm on my own. At break time I just go to the library and read a book. I told my mum about it and she said it wouldn't be this way forever and that Becky will talk to me again one day, but I don't think so.

I tried to talk to Becky before English yesterday and one of the other girls said, "Don't you realize she hates you?" I didn't know what to say after that. Becky looked sort of upset, but she still didn't talk to me. I know when Angel and Julia fell out, Angel felt like that too for a while, but then she found out just in time that Julia was going to be kidnapped by Armenians and they made up. I don't think anything like that will happen to me. On Sunday nights, I feel so terrible that I'm sick. It's the summer holidays soon and that's good, but even then I know that I won't have anyone to talk to and that I'll have to go out on my own and pretend I'm with friends so my mum doesn't worry about me being lonely.

What would Angel do?

Love

Shamilla Choudary xx

Ruby Parker

Dear Shamilla,

I'm sorry that you're feeling so lonely, and I'm sorry it's taken me so long to answer your letter. Today I had a very tough scene at work and I really thought about what Angel would do if she were you. I think that sometimes when there's a whole group of people doing something, it's easier to do what they are than to be different. I think maybe that's what your friend Becky is doing. I don't think she has stopped being your friend—especially not if she was upset about what that nasty girl said to you. Maybe since it's summer now you could ring her up and see her without her other friends around. Or maybe just send her a friendly text message. I bet once the pressure of school is off she'll realize how much she has missed you, because a good friend is hard to find.

If she really has stopped being your friend, well, she really isn't worth being upset about—although I know that's easy to say. I talk to my mum when I'm really worried and I think you should try to talk to your mum again. Ask to her sit down for a minute and really listen. I bet she will, and I bet when she properly understands how sad you are, you'll feel better.

You sound like a lovely girl and I bet you'll make new friends before you know it. If you don't think you can talk to your mum, I have enclosed some leaflets and the number for ChildLine.

Good luck!
Ruby x

Chapter Four

I usually do tell my mum everything. Usually she picks me up from school or the set and we go home together and I tell her all about my day. We laugh and talk about Everest and the things he got up to at home that morning, like trying to kill Mum's fleece, or getting stuck in the cat flap again carrying a whole baguette in his mouth, all nonchalant, like nobody would notice a cat with a baguette. When we'd get in, I'd sit at the table and Mum would make me supper. Then after an hour or so Dad would come in and Mum would say she was off for a bath, and Dad would sit at the table and I'd tell him all about Everest and the baguette, or something else, and he'd tell me a joke he'd heard on the radio. And I'd laugh really loud so Mum could hear us and she'd realize that we *are* happy and that nothing had to change.

When Mum picked me up this afternoon, I really needed to talk to her. But I didn't, because—like Shamilla—I didn't want her to worry about me. I knew if I told her, she'd be lovely, and she'd give me a big hug and we'd sit on the bed and eat chocolate biscuits and somehow she'd make it all right. But I still didn't want to tell her. I didn't want her to worry about anything else. I just wanted to keep on showing her that we *are* happy as a family.

The thing is, if I get dropped from the show, I don't know if I'll be able to go to Sylvia Lighthouse's Academy for the Performing Arts anymore. I mean, I only got in there in the first place because I was on TV. I didn't even have to audition. If I get dropped from the show then maybe I'll get dropped from the school. Maybe everyone, including Sylvia Lighthouse, will see that I haven't got what it takes to make it after all— that maybe I never did.

And it's not as if I'd get another job. I don't think there's work for ugly teenagers *anywhere*. Not even on *EastEnders* anymore. And then I'd lose Nydia and I'd be at a school where everyone would know I was a failure and I wouldn't have any friends and . . .

It's easy to tell other people to be brave and to cheer

up, but it's not so easy to do it yourself. I know I sometimes moan about the school and about starting so early and finishing so late, but I love it. I really, really love it and I don't want to go to a school where everyone has to be good at physics and math and spelling. I'm rubbish at physics and math and spelling.

So I didn't tell Mum because of all that, and also because on the way home she wasn't laughing or smiling and she didn't talk about Everest. In fact, she didn't talk to me at all; she just turned up her Celine Dion CD really loud and pressed her lips together so hard they turned a bit white. She went for a bath before Dad got home, and when he came in, I asked him what his joke of the day was. But he just sat at the table and asked me to give him a big hug.

"I'm so proud of you, Ruby," he said. "You *do* know that, don't you?" And I said that I did, but then I went to bed before it was even eight o'clock, because I know that once he finds out about the show he won't be proud of me anymore. And if he's not proud of me— if he's disappointed in me, if we don't laugh at his jokes every day when he gets in—then what?

Then maybe they'll stop trying for my sake, that's what.

But at least I have Nydia for now. At least, unlike Shamilla, I still have one friend I can talk to. So I phoned Nydia and told her about my day.

"But it's not true!" Nydia said. "There *is* a place for ugly actors on the telly!" And then she sort of coughed and said, "Which you aren't one of anyway. You're beautiful, Ruby, and I'm not just saying that because I'm your friend. I can see that you are beautiful."

"On the inside, you mean?" I asked, glumly.

"Well, yes, but on the outside too. Definitely." And I loved her for saying it, but I knew it wasn't true, not really. On the outside, I'm just almost-average at best—and average isn't good enough.

"The thing is," I told her, "I can't tell Mum and Dad because, well . . . you know. They'll go all bonkers and I can't give them something else to fight about. They've gone ever so quiet lately, Nydia, and they keep hugging me. I think something's going to happen. Something bad." I felt my tummy go cold with fear at the thought of it.

"No, it's not, because we won't let it. I'll think of something, I promise you. I always do, don't I?"

I thought of Nydia's various plans to fix things since I've known her, which included hiding all of the hockey sticks in gym class so we didn't have to play outside in the snow and "build ourselves up for the harsh realities of life in the real world" like our gym teacher, Miss Logan, said. I bit my lip. Nydia's plans usually get us into lunchtime detention for four weeks in a row. Who knows what she might dream up? Some mad plan, I was certain. But I knew she was trying to make me feel better, and just knowing that she cared *did* make me feel better.

I heard a muffled voice on the other end of the line and Nydia shouted right in my ear, "All right, Mum, I'm coming! Listen, Ruby, I've got to go. Gran's here. I'll ring you back after dinner, OK? Even if it's ten or something, and we'll talk then. But don't worry, Ruby. You're a really great actress *and* you're pretty, and I'm not just saying it, OK?"

After she'd gone, I flicked through the numbers on my mobile looking for someone else to talk to, but I don't have very many numbers on it—just one for this French girl I met on holiday last Easter, and for Nydia, Mum, Dad, and Gran. I thought about calling my gran, but she's a bit deaf and she'd probably ask me to repeat everything twice, really loudly, and she'd end up thinking I was asking her about the war or something.

Then I looked at Brett's name. I remembered the day she put her number in my mobile. It was the first day I got it and I was showing it to everyone and feeling really cool. Brett took it from me and put in her home number and she said, right in front of the journalist who was interviewing her, "You know you're like a daughter to me, don't you, darling? Any time you need to talk, you just call me. Any time, sweetie."

So I did.

I was a bit nervous about calling her because she's such a big star, the *real* star of the show, the one who goes on all the chat shows and the only one who's published an autobiography about her affair with a footballer. When I'm being Angel and she's being my mum, sometimes it's like having a little holiday from my life. It's not that I don't love my mum or my dad, it's just that, when Brett's being my mum and I'm being Angel, all of the things we say and all of our problems have been written out for us. I don't have to worry that anything I say or do might make things worse or more difficult. I don't have to worry because I know it all will be OK in the end. Brett is very good at being Angel's mum. She always makes Angel feel loved and better, and when Angel feels better, then so do I.

So I called her.

"Yes?" Brett said. She sounded a bit cross, as if she thought I was someone else—the press, probably. The press is always hounding Brett; she's always giving interviews about it.

"Brett? Hello, it's me." There was a long pause. "It's

41

Ruby—er, from the show?" There was another pause and I thought I heard the clatter of a glass or something.

"Now, Ruby, I don't know what you've heard, but . . ."

"Oh. You know, then? Does everyone?" I felt my insides shrivel up. I couldn't face having to go back to work and see Justin, knowing that he knew and everything.

"Er, know what, exactly, darling?" Brett asked me.

"About me being dropped from the show. Being killed for being ugly." I explained what I'd overheard. And the minute I finished speaking, Brett's voice changed completely. Once she understood how bad I felt, she was just like Angel's mum, soft and understanding.

"Oh, darling, how ghastly," she said. "I hadn't heard that. It comes as a total shock! It must have been terrible for you. What monsters! What do they know, crushing a young girl's spirits like that? And it's simply not true, darling! I've always said you have wonderful bones. And I used to be a model, so I know."

I wasn't exactly sure what use it was having wonderful bones that no one could see, but when Brett said it, then it felt important. So I started to tell her about how worried I was about school, and about my mum and dad. I found that once I started to tell her one thing, I wanted to tell her everything, just like Angel would have.

"The thing is, darling," she interrupted me, "I've got a really early shoot tomorrow and I have to be on the set at four A.M.! God knows what they expect me to look like at that hour. But don't you worry, OK? Brett won't let this happen without having her say! I don't know how much influence I'll have, Ruby, but I'll talk to Liz first thing and try to make her understand. I promise."

"Oh, thank you. Thank you, Brett," I told her. "It's just that I don't want to worry Mum and—"

"Of course not, dear." Then Brett paused, as if she'd just thought of something. "Ruby, are you on the set tomorrow?"

"No, I'm off," I said.

"Well then, leave it to me, dear. Leave it to me. Kisses!"

And then she was gone.

It took me a long time to get to sleep, even knowing that Brett was going to help me. Somehow being away from the set when something so important was being decided about me seemed worse than if I were actually there going through it.

At least Nydia called me back, just before I went to sleep.

And she did have a plan.

And it *was* a mad one.

Chapter Five

I t's very simple," Nydia said the next afternoon as she unpacked the contents of her bag onto my bed. "They don't think you're pretty enough, right?"

"Right." I rolled my eyes.

"Sooooo . . ." Nydia held up a packet of Blonde Beauty permanent hair dye. "We'll show them. We'll make you over today! When you go in there tomorrow, you'll knock their socks off and they won't kill you. OK?"

I shook my head in disbelief. "*Oh*, no. No, no, no, no! You aren't getting anywhere near me with that. My hair will go all green and fall out! Haven't you ever seen *Hollyoaks*, *Neighbours*, or *Family Affairs*? It *always* goes wrong—especially when you're thirteen. No. No way."

I crossed my arms and tried to look stern, which is hard with Nydia because she always makes me laugh by rolling her eyes and crossing them.

"I knew you'd say that," she said with a sigh. "You're the one who tells me off for believing in happy endings and yet you believe all the *bad* stuff that happens on the telly. You're the same as me, just in reverse. It's only a soap, love! Anyway, knowing how terrible you are at rebelling, I brought you this instead." She held up a lemon. "I read about it in a magazine. We squeeze it in your hair, sit in the garden for the whole afternoon, and the sun will turn your hair blonde again. Good thing there's global warming. It's really hot out there. And then when we've done that, we'll pluck your eyebrows. Don't look at me like that! It's easy; I've got a magazine article about it. Then we'll do your makeup and find *something* cool in your wardrobe. It's just a shame you don't wear glasses, because then we could get you some contact lenses and everyone would be like, 'Wow!'"

I took the lemon from her and slumped down on my bed.

"I don't think your plan is going to work, Nydia," I said.

"Yes it will! And if not, it could still make you feel better; at least it will take your mind off things for a bit." She wrapped her arms around me and gave me a big hug. "I'm sorry, Ruby. I *did* try to think of a plan that would really help, but the only other thing I could think of was storming the ten o'clock news and holding an on-air protest, which I think just might make things worse. Obviously one day I'll be a mega-superstar and everyone will do what I say, but, until then, this was the best I could come up with. Don't you think lemon in your hair might make you feel better?"

I hugged her and looked at the lemon. "*You* make me feel better," I said, smiling at her. "Come on, let's go and squeeze this and I'll try not to worry anymore."

We walked out onto the landing and Mum was there, just standing there holding her hands together really tightly. She sort of jumped when she saw us.

"Oh," she said, trying to sound cheerful. "Um, do you want anything, girls? A drink or a snack or something?"

I looked at Nydia, who shook her head.

"No thanks, Mrs. Parker," she said with her best parents' smile.

Mum nodded while knitting and unknitting her fingers. "Um, Nydia, were you planning to stay for dinner?" she asked. "It's just that, well, today's not the best day . . ."

"Mum!" I protested. It wasn't like her not to let Nydia stay for as long as she liked, and I really needed Nydia to help me keep my mind off everything. And besides, I felt like while she was here nothing else could happen. "Why not?"

Mum looked at me anxiously, and then looked back at Nydia.

"Because your father and I want to talk to you," she said, and I knew it was something bad. Whenever she refers to my dad as "your father," it's bad—like when Granddad died or when Dad went away last year and stayed in a hotel for a week to "think about things."

"What about?" I asked her. "What's happened, Mum?"

Mum shook her head and pressed her lips together again. "We'll talk later, OK? Don't worry. There'll be plenty of other times for Nydia to come to dinner." She was blinking a lot as she said it. "You don't mind, do you, Nydia?"

Nydia shook her head; her smile had faded. "No. I don't mind, Mrs. Parker. No worries!" She looked at me and bit her lip.

"Right, well, I'll bring you some biscuits, then?"

"Will you squeeze this for us?" I held out the lemon. I felt stupid asking, but Mum nodded and took it, turning her back to me as we headed to the kitchen.

"That's it, isn't it?" I said after we had squeezed the lemon in my hair. "It has to be. Their marriage is over."

Nydia took my hand and led me down the stairs and into the garden. "Maybe not," she said as we sat down on the grass. "Maybe it's the trial separation again, or maybe they're going to sell the house because your dad's got a secret gambling addiction or something . . ."

"That's from the show!" I said with half a smile. I looked around the garden and listened to the bees in the grass and the sound of the neighbors' toddler in the paddling pool, and I shut my eyes tightly for a second and waited for the tears to go back inside my head.

"*I* know," I said to Nydia. "Let's talk about the film we're writing; we still haven't thought of a really good ending. So far we've only got up to the bit where Justin and I are in the jungle lair of the evil alien who's about to take over the world . . ."

And for the next couple of hours we acted like nothing bad was going to happen. Luckily for me, we're really good at acting.

3 Briar Walk
Berkhamsted
Herts HP4 3BL

Dear Angel,

You are so brave. I wish I was as brave as you were when you tripped up that trained assassin trying to kill your uncle and bashed him over the head with a priceless antique vase. You saved your uncle's life! I really think he should have been more grateful and worried less about the vase.

I am not brave. I am scared of most things. Dogs, spiders, the dark, thunder, and cheese. But I can't say I am because all my friends would laugh and call me a baby. So if I see a dog or a spider, I just pretend not to be scared and try to be brave like Angel, even though I'm not really.

Lots of love,
Lucy James (age 11)

Dear Lucy,

Thank you for your letter, but I think you are a bit wrong actually. I think you are very brave indeed. I know grown-ups (my mum) who are so scared of spiders they can't even stay in the same room with them!

It's easy to be brave when I'm playing Angel because she isn't afraid of anything. In real life I'm afraid of a lot of things, just like you, and I bet your friends are too. Why don't you ask them the next time you have a sleepover? Anyway, from now on, if I'm worried and scared, I'm going to think about you and try to be just as brave as you are!

Best wishes,
Ruby x

Chapter Six

I knew when I went down to dinner that I was going to have to be as brave as Lucy, maybe even braver. It was bound to be bad because Mum made chicken risotto, and she only makes that when we have guests or if I'm sick or something, because it takes her hours and she has to stir it until her wrists go funny.

I sat at the table and watched her stir and stir, her face tipped down into the steam as if she could see something else apart from risotto in the saucepan. Everest sat at her feet and gazed up, trying his best to psychically levitate some of the chicken out of the pan and into his paws.

"What is it, Mum?" I finally asked her. I was pulling

my fingers through my hair, which, although it smelled nice, was not any blonder than it had been this morning.

Mum looked up at me and smiled, but it was one of those upside-down smiles that are really more like frowns—like a mixture of both the comic and the tragic mask in my school badge. "Dad will be here in a minute and then we'll talk about things," she told me carefully. "We just need to talk, Ruby—about how things are at the moment and how things are going to be."

I felt my stomach knot up and tighten again. When she said *things*, she meant *us*. She meant me and Mum and Dad and how *we* were going to be.

"Things are fine, though," I said, trying to stay casual, as if a nameless dread wasn't beginning to boil up again in my tummy. In the garden with Nydia—in the middle of our film, in the middle of the jungle with Justin swinging me through the trees on vines to save us from giant man-eating ants—my tummy knots had untied themselves and gone away. I told myself that I'd been worrying over nothing—that I was exaggerating the way I was feeling again and getting everything out of proportion, like I did when I thought this lump on my foot was cancer and it turned out to be an insect bite. But even if it hadn't been for the chicken risotto, I knew that what was coming was bad when I heard

Mum's voice. When she spoke, her voice sounded as if it was stretched very, very thinly, as if she were speaking from a very long way off. Another universe, practically.

And then Dad came in and Mum went sort of stiff and nobody looked at me for a long time. They went about just doing normal stuff, only it wasn't normal because normally they weren't ever in the same room as long as this. Dad hung up his coat and took off his tie. Mum put out the cutlery and poured out drinks and didn't ask me to do anything, which was *definitely* not normal. And neither one of them told Everest off for sitting right wherever it was they were trying to walk and for making them trip and stumble. Dad didn't even tell me his joke of the day. They just moved around like robots.

Then we all sat at the table and Mum brought out the food. I looked at it steaming on my plate; it looked delicious, but somehow not real, and I couldn't eat any. My stomach was too full up with worry.

"Ruby, do you want some cheese?" Mum passed me the shaker, but I pushed it away. I couldn't stand this abnormal normalness for a minute longer.

"Just say it!" I snapped. My words popped the bubble of tension that had suffocated the room like cling film, and suddenly the kitchen was crowded with emotion.

"Just say whatever it is you're going to say. Please. Just say it."

I felt frightened then, and very small. Mum and Dad looked at each other and there was a moment of silence. I felt Everest come and sit on my feet; his fat, warm body made my toes tickle, and I told myself it was because he was on my side and not because he was just after scraps.

"Well . . . ," Mum said, looking at Dad. "You tell her, Frank. I think that it's you who should tell her."

The way my dad looked at my mum then—I've never seen him look at her, or anyone, like that before. He looked at her as if he didn't even know her, like she was just some strange woman in his house telling him what to do. He looked at her as if he didn't like her, not even a little bit.

"Ruby, you know that things have been difficult at home for a while, don't you?"

I shook my head vigorously. Just like Mum, he was talking about *things* again. Why didn't he say what he meant? Why didn't he talk about me, Mum, us? We're not *things*. We're living, breathing people.

"No. No, I don't know that. I think *things* have been fine. Really fine," I said. "So don't worry about me. I'm *fine*. Is that all?"

Dad bit his lip and took a deep breath. He picked

up his fork and put it down again. Then he swallowed as if someone had made him take some really bad medicine. I watched his face for any sign of what it was he was about to say, but it was almost as if my dad wasn't in there.

"Ruby, I'm sorry," he spoke at last. "Your mum and I, we don't get along like we used to. We've been making each other . . . unhappy . . . for a long time now."

My mum huffed out a breath of air, as if "unhappy" wasn't nearly a good enough word to describe how my dad made her feel.

I looked at them both, from one to the other. My mum and dad: the two people who put me here in the world. It was them loving each other in the first place that made me happen. If they hated each other, then what about me? Did they hate me too?

I tried to make them see that we *were* happy. "Are you sure?" I asked quickly. "Because I don't think we're as unhappy as you think we are. I mean, when you say a long time, how long do you mean? We were happy at Christmas, weren't we? And that's only a few months ago. We were happy on holiday. We're a little happy every day, aren't we?"

Neither one of them would look at me.

"Well, aren't we?" I pressed on. "It's about working it out, isn't it? And anyway, you *don't* make each other unhappy. Mum, didn't Dad get you that perfume you really wanted at Christmas? And you were happy then, weren't you? And you're happy when Mum makes a big roast, aren't you, Dad? You love a big roast, don't you?"

Mum looked at her hands.

"Well?" I asked them both.

Mum reached across the table and picked up my hand; her skin felt hot and dry. "We were, darling, but you'll understand better when you're a bit older. Being happy for one day a year, or just sometimes—it's not enough." She shut her eyes tightly for a second and then looked at me. "And sometimes . . . sometimes it's easier to *pretend* to be happy."

I shook my head in disbelief. Mum was holding my hand, but it felt like I was slipping away from her, from Dad, from everything I knew and trusted about my life, into an unknown darkness.

"No, you see, that's not right. And anyway, it's a start, isn't it?" I looked at Dad, desperate to make him see. "Because you used to be happy every day, and if you used to be, you could be again."

I sat up and reached out my other hand to Dad so I was linking the two of them together. "I know there are rocky patches, but I think we'll be OK. I really do." I smiled at them both. "I really, really do, but I'm glad we've talked about it and it's all out in the open so all we have to do now is—"

"Ruby, I'm leaving." Dad spoke over me. The words dropped onto the table with a clatter like heavy stones. "I'm not going to live in the house anymore."

As I stared at him, my smile gradually fell and melted away. "You mean for a bit, like before?" My voice was very small. "While you clear your head and have space?" I asked him hopefully.

Dad shook his head and moved his hand away from under mine. "No, darling. I mean I've got a new place—a little flat. It's only five minutes away, but I'm going to live there. I'm going to take some stuff and sleep there tonight and move out over the next few days. But, Ruby, you must understand; it's not *you* I'm leaving. It's just the house . . . it's just . . ." He looked at my mum, who had turned her face away from us, as if she couldn't bear to look at him; her skin looked like it had turned to hard, cold, gray rock. "It's not you that I'm leaving. I'll still be your dad, I'll see you just as much, more even, and—"

"NO!" I screamed. And just then, everything—all the fear and the worry and the knowing—welled right up inside me like a volcano and erupted. I pushed back my chair so hard it fell over with a clatter and Everest shot out from under the table, yowling, and raced through the cat flap.

"No!" I shouted again, slamming my hands down on the tabletop and making my palms sting. "No, Dad, it won't be the same. How will it be the same? How can you even say that? How can you say that you're going, tell me that you've known you were going for ages? You've just let me go around thinking I have a normal life, a life with proper parents. People's mums and dads live together; that's how it's supposed to be. Otherwise why did you ever get married? Why did you ever have me?"

Then I looked at my mum and waited until she looked back at me. I felt so angry with her, just sitting there made out of stone, not doing anything. "Why are you letting him do this, Mum? Why don't you *do* something? You could have been nicer to him, been kinder or something, been pleased when he got you flowers instead of going on about your hay fever. Or happy when he got you chocolates instead of cross because of your diet. Why are you letting him do this? Why are you driving him away?"

Mum shook her head and looked like she was trying to say something, but her mouth just moved and no words came out. I could see her body was trembling, and her gray skin suddenly flared up with blotches of bright red and she began to cry. She held out her arms to me.

"Oh, baby, sometimes there's nothing *anyone* can do. I'm so sorry, Ruby, I . . ."

I wanted to go to her then and sit on her lap and hug her like I used to when I was a baby, but I didn't. I couldn't. I had to make them see what they were doing. "No! You're just giving up! Why are you giving up? There is *always* something you can do! You—both of you—just don't care! You don't care about what happens to me, do you? You don't even love me anymore; you can't if you're going to do *this*!"

I ran out the back door and into the garden. I found Everest hiding on the swing seat, and I picked him up and hugged him so hard that he struggled for a bit and tried to get away. But then I think he felt my tears wet his fur and he stopped and sort of snuggled close to me and rested his soft, fat head on my shoulder and stared at me.

"They don't know what they're doing, Everest," I told him between sobs. "They think they know, but they don't." I cried and cried then, quietly, into Everest's fur.

It was a long time before Dad came outside. The sun had gradually seeped from the sky, leaving traces of its light streaking the evening. When he opened the back door, a rectangle of yellow fell over the grass and I could see his silhouette, but not his face. I'd worked out what to say to him; I knew exactly what to say to make him stay. Dad always gave in to me in the end because we were best friends. When Mum made up her mind about something, it stayed made up, but Dad was the sort of person you could talk to and reason with. I'd always believed that he loved me—that whatever he said about Mum, he'd never want to hurt me.

I waited until he walked across the grass and sat down next to me on the swing. Everest opened one eye and looked at him. Dad put his arm around my shoulder and tried to hug me, but I held myself very stiff, so he just rested his hand there instead.

"Darling, I know this is hard for you," he said, sounding like my dad again and not the stranger who'd been in the kitchen. "I know right now you can't see how this is ever going to be OK, but one day, when you're a bit older, you'll understand . . ."

I wanted to hug him, but I shrugged his hand off my shoulder and slid away from him. "A bit older? Why? Why doesn't anything I think or feel matter *now*? Why doesn't it, Dad?"

He shook his head. "Of course it does, Ruby. Of course it matters. All I'm saying is right now you can't see things the way your mum and I can . . ." Dad trailed off as if he had run out of words.

My moment had come. I slid Everest off my lap and onto the cushioned seat of the swing and I picked up Dad's hand. This was my big scene; these were the lines I'd been rehearsing out here all this time as the sun went down.

"Dad, please. I love you so much and I don't want you to live in some poky little flat. I want you to live at home with me. Stay, Dad, *please*. If you love me, please, stay for me."

I'd been certain—I was *sure*—that if *I* asked him, he would stay. He would hug me and sigh and say, "Of course, Ruby. Of course I'll stay because I do love you."

But he didn't. He just shook his head and said, "I'm really sorry, Ruby, but I can't. I have to go."

Chapter Seven

After Dad had said that he was going anyway, no matter how I felt, he got up and walked back to the house. A sort of numbness spread through me, and I stayed outside in the garden until the last bit of warmth of the day had finally gone, waiting to feel something again. Finally, I went to the kitchen door. I couldn't see Mum or Dad, so I went inside.

I just wanted to go upstairs, get into bed, pull the duvet over my head, and go to sleep and forget about everything. But Mum was in the living room and she heard me.

"Ruby?" The tight voice she'd had earlier seemed to have snapped and disintegrated, and I knew she'd been crying too. I stood outside the doorway for a moment and I wished more than anything that I didn't have to go in there and see her crying. But I went in anyway.

"Are you OK?" I asked. I didn't sound like I meant it. I couldn't seem to feel anything at all—just numbness like I'd been swimming in cold water for too long. And I think I even sounded a bit cold, maybe angry with her still.

She sat up in the armchair and wiped the heel of her hand across her eyes. "Yes, darling, I'm OK. I feel sad, Ruby—hurt and angry and sad, but I'll be OK. *We* will be OK, I promise you."

She tried to smile, and held out a hand to me, so I took it and sat on the arm of the chair, although at that moment all I wanted to do was run upstairs and hide under the duvet.

"What's worrying me is you, Ruby. All this, everything that's happened this evening—this isn't how I thought it would be. Your dad and I thought we were protecting you by trying to sort things out before telling you. We thought if we all sat down and talked it through it would be easier for you. I can see now that it must have been a terrible shock. I . . . I suppose I thought you sort of already knew, that you were expecting it. We didn't do a very good job and I'm sorry, Ruby. I really am. We were trying to think of you, but we got it wrong."

Like everything else, I wanted to say, but I didn't.

She put her arm around my waist and hugged me close to her.

"Mum, did you want Dad to go?" I asked her tentatively. "Was this your idea too?"

She bit her lip hard and looked up at me with red-rimmed eyes. Her mascara had spread out over her face and cheeks.

"No, darling," she said. "I didn't want him to go. But I also know I can't stop him from going—not without hurting us all even more. I know that eventually this will be for the best and we're going to try very hard to make this OK for you. We didn't get off to a good start, but we will make it work. We're not going to fight over you; you can see him whenever you want. You can even live with him if you want . . ."

The way she said it made it clear that if I did, it would hurt her more than anything. Even if I had wanted to live with Dad, I couldn't. I couldn't leave Mum because I loved her. I understood that, even if Dad didn't.

I shook my head. "I don't want to live with him," I said. "And I don't want to live with you. I want to live with us, all together, like always."

Mum sighed and her shoulders slumped. She looked exhausted. "It's going to take a long time to get used to it, Ruby, but we will . . ." she said, rubbing her closed eyes with her fingertips.

"But if it hadn't been for Dad, you'd have kept on trying, wouldn't you?" I asked her, thinking again of Dad's refusal to stay, even for me.

Mum thought for a moment. "Yes . . ." She hesitated. "I probably would have, but if your dad didn't feel the same, it wouldn't have worked. It couldn't have. It's no one's fault. Ruby, you mustn't blame—"

"But it *is* him!" I interrupted with a flash of anger. "He doesn't love us anymore, Mum. It's not that he needs space, or that he wants to be on his own. He just doesn't want us. It's not just you; it's me too. This is all his fault."

Mum shook her head. "No, Rube, that's not true—" she began, but I couldn't listen to her anymore. I didn't want her to stop me from feeling angry. If I was angry, I wasn't hurt; I wasn't lost and I wasn't abandoned. Angry was much, *much* better.

I stood up. "But it is—it *is* true." I raised my voice and gestured toward the garden. "Because he told me it was, out there. So you needn't worry; I don't want to live with him. I don't even want to see him or speak to him ever again."

And then at last I did run up the stairs, climb into bed, pull the duvet over my head, and shut my eyes as tightly as I could. But I couldn't stop the tears from squeezing out. After a while, I just cried. I cried for a long time and thought about Mum downstairs crying somewhere too, and him out there probably laughing his head off, and I couldn't believe that anything that had happened to me today was real. How *could* it be real? How can a person's life change so completely over a few short days? And worse still, it was nothing like on *Kensington Heights*. There was no one there to rewrite the script, bring in a rich uncle or an identical twin, and make sure it all turns out OK in the end.

"Are you sure he's not coming back?" Nydia asked when I called her, still under my duvet.

"I'm sure," I said staunchly. "And I'm glad. I don't want him to come back. Ever."

Nydia thought for a moment. "Maybe we could do something like in that film *The Parent Trap*, about the twins who have to get their mum and dad back together again. I could think of a plan. Hey, maybe we could get them trapped in a lift or something."

I smiled because Nydia was always so sure that her plans would work. "It's a good idea, but it won't work—not this time. It's all right, really. I mean, OK, so my career is over and I'm only thirteen, I come from a broken home and, oh yeah, I'll never have a boyfriend because I'm the frumpiest girl in Britain, and I'll probably get chucked out of the academy and have to go to school without you. But apart from that, everything is just fine." It seemed easier to joke about than to actually think about it.

"You might get a boyfriend one day," Nydia said, trying her best. "I wouldn't rule it out totally." And I knew that Nydia couldn't think of anything else to say when she said, "Yeah, and on the bright side, things can't get any worse."

Want to bet?

Chapter Eight

Mum told me I didn't have to go to the studio the next morning. She said she'd ring in and that Liz would understand, but I said that I needed to go. I didn't tell her that, after this morning, I didn't think I'd be going for very much longer.

I just needed to get out of the house because it was so strange without Dad there, without him drinking his coffee on the way out of the house and leaving his mug on the gatepost. It was strange without his coat on the hook on the back of the kitchen door next to Mum's and mine like it always had been, or without last night's paper folded up on his favorite chair. So I had to go even though I knew Mum didn't want me to—maybe

69

because she didn't want me to, and even though I was sure this would be the day they would fire me.

Just then, it felt like too much for me to be strong for her. I haven't worked out how to be strong for myself yet. I think it's probably best to try not to think about it at all and just to think about everything else. There certainly was a lot to think about.

It was quiet when I got to the studio; everyone else had been up early doing a night shoot before the morning rehearsal. (Minors like me don't do that stuff a lot. We're only allowed to work a set amount of hours a week, in case it turns into slave labor.) Vera, the canteen lady, made me a bacon roll and a cup of tea and I went to the rehearsal room, hoping it would still be empty. But Brett was there.

"Hi, Brett," I said. I was surprised how my voice came out, all small and sad; in my head I'd been bright and breezy. I didn't want anyone to know about Dad leaving. I wanted everything here to be normal . . . until they fired me, that is.

Brett glanced up from her script and she looked furious. But the moment she saw me, she quickly rearranged her face into a smile.

"Are you OK?" I asked her tentatively. Brett sometimes has these "artistic episodes" when suddenly she can just go off, and anyone in the way will do as a target. She'd never targeted me before—what with me practically being like a daughter to her—but I suppose there could always be a first time, especially with the luck I'd been having. And then I realized: It must be because she's tried to talk to Liz about not firing me but she'd failed.

"I'm fine, darling, fine," Brett said through gritted teeth. "OK, sometimes I wonder what on earth it is I'm doing in this flea circus, when no one listens to what I say. After all, who am *I*?" Her voice was gradually increasing in volume. "I'm only the person who everyone switches on to see, the one they come back to watch, week after week. What do I count?"

Luckily, just as I thought I might have to try to answer her, Liz, Martin, Justin, and the rest of the cast for that morning came in.

"Brett," Liz said with extra patience, just like my next-door neighbor does when her toddler has a tantrum, "is there *still* a problem? I thought we had resolved this."

Brett rolled her eyes and leaned back in her chair, tossing her blonde hair so that the darker roots showed for a second.

"There's no problem," she said, making it perfectly clear that somehow there was. As Brett lowered her voice to talk to Liz, I took the opportunity to scoot past them and sit in the farthest corner of the room, hoping that no one would notice me and consequently not fire me. (This plan would have backfired, mind you, when I had to start reading my lines.)

"Ah, Ruby!" Liz gave me her shiniest smile. "I'm going to need to chat with you afterward, OK? I've got some fantastic news!"

I looked at Brett, whose face seemed to have folded in on itself with anger. Fantastic. She's going to try to make it sound great that they're chucking me off the show, just like Mum and Dad tried to make it sound like it's the best thing ever that they've split up. What is it with adults? Why can't they just admit it when bad things happen? Why don't they just all agree that, actually, thanks very much, things *couldn't* be worse?

"Er, OK," I said glumly, sinking as far down in my chair as I could without actually falling off it. I had to wait until after read-through and my two lines for Liz to give me the "fantastic news."

The rehearsal went well, like a normal day, really. First we did a read-through—just read the words like we're reciting from the phone book or something.

72

That's when the main actors ask questions about motivation, make notes on the scripts, or change their lines slightly. Then we read again, sort of half acting this time, so we save the best until we're on the set. It all went like clockwork.

"Right, that was great, everyone," Liz said, clapping her hands together and bouncing a little bit so that her jewelry jangled. "Really felt the energy in the room today. Just before you go for filming, I've got a couple of things I want to say."

I felt my cheeks begin to smolder with the beginnings of a blush. I couldn't believe she was going to announce it in front of everyone—especially in front of Justin! I tried to look at him while I still had the chance, but he'd let his fringe flop over his eyes this morning and he was looking far too beautiful for me to be able to properly stare at him. So I just braced myself for the final humiliation.

"I want you all to meet Danny," Liz said instead. "Come in, Dan!"

My head snapped up and my jaw dropped. It was Danny—Danny Harvey from school. He looked around the room and, when he caught my eye, raised an eyebrow and half smiled at me. I was so surprised I just sort of blinked back at him like I had grit in my eye. By the time I'd managed to smile back he was his usual scowling self again.

Liz dropped her arm around Danny's shoulder and gave him a squeeze. "Danny will be joining the cast for the rest of this season's shooting, playing the part of Marcus Ridely, Caspian's bad-influence younger cousin."

Everyone smiled and waved at Danny and said something along the lines of "welcome" and "hello." He just about managed to smile back but, unlike Justin, who can walk into a room and just know that everybody loves him, Danny looked a bit awkward. He even sort of blushed a little, which is something they would never believe at school. Danny is really cool there. He's *so* not the sort of boy who blushes.

As everyone filed out for a quick break before filming, I made my way over to Danny. I wanted to be nice to him because he seemed a bit lost and I knew how it felt to stick out somewhere and not quite fit in.

"Hi," I said to Danny. He sort of shrugged back a hello and looked at the floor.

"Hi," he said.

"So, you never said you were coming on the show," I said.

He shrugged again and looked at the door this time.

"I didn't know," he said to the door. "Didn't find out until later on. There were all these auditions. I didn't want to say anything in case I didn't get it and I'd look like a loser, like Michael Henderson did when he said he was definitely going to be on *The Bill* and they picked that other kid from *Grange Hill* . . ." He trailed off and looked around the room—everywhere, I realized, except at me.

"Yeah, that was pretty funny," I said with a last attempt at a smile. Danny looked like he'd really rather I left him alone and stopped forcing him to speak to me. At school the only times he's ever properly spoken to me was when Nydia was out sick and we had to do a chemistry experiment together, and then when we both got put on tea-and-biscuits duty at the Parents' Open Day. And even then all he did for two whole hours was describe how to build an electric guitar. Like, big wow, he's so interesting. Come to think of it, he never actually looked at me then, either. Why should it be any different here?

"So!" Liz bounded up to us. She does bound sometimes, despite being over fifty and quite heavy. Lots of her sort of jiggles when she does this, but she doesn't seem to mind at all. "You two know each other already from school, don't you? I wasn't allowed to mention

Danny to you, Ruby. He was determined to get the part on his own without anyone putting a word in." She patted Danny rather firmly on the back.

"I wouldn't have put a word in," I said before thinking. "I mean, it wouldn't have mattered if I had or not. I'm not important at all, am I, Liz?" I looked at Danny, but he seemed to have hunched up his shoulders so much that his head had practically disappeared between them.

"Oh, but you *are* important," Liz said with a smile. "Danny, do you mind, I just need a quick chat with Ruby here . . ."

Danny more or less ran out of the room like he couldn't wait to get as far away from me as possible. I looked at Liz and waited.

"Well," Liz began with a deep breath, "I didn't want to tell you this before, but we had a meeting about you the other day, Ruby—about where you're going and how you're developing."

I nodded, only just managing not to say, "I know."

"Well, we love you, Ruby. We think you just light up the screen!"

Talk about softening the blow.

"And so we've decided to bring your character forward through the rest of this season and build your part up so that by next year, when you're a bit older, you'll really be ready to get involved in some big story lines."

I stared at Liz and opened my mouth, waiting for something to come out.

"But . . . ?" was all that came out. I looked over at Brett, who was watching us closely. It must have been her; it must have been Brett who had convinced Liz to let me stay. When Liz said something about the problem and how she thought it was all over, she must have been talking about *me*. Brett must have just gotten so angry in defending me that it was taking her a long time to come out of it. Brett is a Method actress and frequently stays in character for a long time after filming is over, like she did when Angel's mum was drunk all the time. It must be something like that. I wanted to run over and hug her, but she still looked quite scary, so I didn't.

"So, the scripts are being edited now, but I wanted to give you a taste of where we're going with them so you can be as excited as we are," Liz continued. "You know that Angel has had this crush on Caspian forever and used to follow him around? Well, we thought it would be fun if Angel decides she needs to show him she's growing up now. We thought we might do your hair a bit, Ruby, and get you a few new items for the wardrobe. A bit of lip gloss, too. I'll have to talk it over with your mum, but just something a bit more grown up." I nodded, still dumbfounded. "And so then we thought, wouldn't it be lovely if Caspian realized that Angel was turning into a beauty *and*—you'll love this—gives Angel her first kiss! It won't be anything heavy, of course, hardly more than a peck, but . . ."

And that was the last thing I heard her say.

Chapter Nine

What's worse than getting fired from the show?

Not getting fired from the show. Not getting fired from the show and being told you're getting your very own story line.

"What's the problem?" you ask. "You should be jumping for joy!" OK, try this—*not* getting fired from the show and being told you're getting your own story line about Angel telling Caspian that she loves him! Still don't get it? Story line culminates in Angel's *very first ever kiss*—with Caspian!

Which is *my very first ever kiss* with *anyone*. And it's *not* just anyone anyway. It's *Justin*, who I am so in love with that I nearly *die* when I look at him, never mind if I actually had to *kiss* him!

I mean, I'm glad I'm not getting fired from the show. Of course I am. It's just that when I was sure it was going to happen, it seemed so important, as if it was linked up with the rest of my life. As if Mum and Dad being together and me being Angel were all somehow linked. And so after Dad left, I was ready for it. I was even a little bit relieved.

"I didn't see this coming," I said after I'd filled Nydia in on the news. She looked as shocked as I felt.

"Hang on a minute. Let me look at your stars," Nydia said, pulling her mum's copy of *Cosmopolitan* out from under the bed. I looked at the cover as she flicked through the pages. "Teens who have plastic surgery!" was one of the articles listed on the cover. I wondered if that was why Nydia had taken it; she was always going on about having liposuction. And even if she *was* just joking, she read and watched anything she could find on the subject with dogged curiosity. It might have been that, or "101 Ways to Increase Your Cleavage," although Nydia didn't seem bothered about the size of her bust. What about ways to decrease your cleavage? After all, how am I even going to be able to kiss Justin in the first place if I can't get close enough to him to make lip contact, what with the Breasts getting in the way and everything. And then there's the whole nose and mouth placement and . . . and . . . and . . .

"Just as I thought," Nydia said, distracting me before I dissolved into a puddle of panic. She read from the magazine: "Aries—you'll find yourself on a real roller-coaster ride this week as your emotions are pulled in a hundred different directions. Just hold on and everything will be all right, maybe even better than you imagined."

"Ha!" I said without much enthusiasm.

Nydia tracked her finger down the page to her own star sign. "Gemini—nothing ever happens to you. Get over it." She read it deadpan, pulling down the corners of her mouth.

"It doesn't say that!" I laughed despite my panic and grabbed the magazine out of her hand just to double-check.

"No, it doesn't," she agreed, with a sigh. She crossed her legs and propped her chin in her hands. "But it might as well. Nothing ever happens to me."

I put *Cosmo* down and looked at her. "Nydia, I'd do anything to swap your life for mine. At least *you* have a proper family that actually likes one another. Your mum and dad even still hold hands when you go out . . ."

Nydia rolled her eyes. "Ugh, I know. It's so disgusting . . ." she began, but then saw the look on my face

81

and stopped. "I'm sorry, Ruby. I know you're having a tough week—like the toughest week ever in the history of your life." She thought for a moment. "Actually, I'm surprised your mum even let you come over tonight. I didn't expect to see you all week. I thought you'd be 'talking it through.'" Nydia made air quotes with her fingers.

I thought about the look on my mum's face when I asked her to drop me off at Nydia's instead of taking me home after I'd finished at the studio.

"But I'd thought that we could have something nice for dinner—Chinese or something. What do you say?" She sounded sort of desperate and hopeful—not how a mum should sound at all. It scared me. "And then we could talk about things," she'd continued. "We haven't had a chance to talk about much really, have we, darling? I'm worried about you. About how you're handling this . . ."

I'd looked out of the car window and watched the dirt gray streets as we crawled our way home through the rush-hour traffic. "But there's nothing to talk about, is there?" I'd said bluntly. "I mean, it's already happened. You and Dad decided it and now it's done." I thought of Dad walking out on me in the garden. "What I felt didn't matter, so I'd really rather just get *on* with things now, Mum, and try to forget about it, because nothing I say or do is going to make any difference, is it? What I feel doesn't really matter, does it?"

I looked back at her then and saw the look of sorrow on her face as she tried to think of something to say. I knew that I should just go home. I knew I should be with her and let her see that I was all right and that she hadn't done something *so* terrible to me that I would never get over it. But I couldn't; I didn't feel like that. I didn't feel OK. I didn't feel like being brave and I didn't feel strong enough to be there for *her* to lean on *me*. It was too much. *Much* too much.

I was supposed to be the child. *I* was supposed to be the one who did the leaning on both of my parents. But last night they had just pulled that rug out from under my feet without thinking.

So I'd just looked out the window again at the passing blur of traffic and said, "Nydia's dad will drive me home before ten."

"She's feeling guilty, so she's letting me out of all the 'talking it through,'" I said to Nydia.

"OK, then let's try to put the negative aside," she said. "We should just focus on the positive." Nydia tucked her legs underneath her and clapped her hands together. "After all, you're going to kiss the love of your life! *Ohmygodhowexcitingisthat!*"

I felt a sudden rush of adrenaline surge through me and fizz in the tips of my fingers and toes. Just the thought that the dream that sent me off to sleep every night might actually come true made me feel like floating a couple of inches above Nydia's bed.

And then it was as if I was on the roller coaster *Cosmo* had predicted, and my stomach plummeted toward my feet.

"I feel sick," I said.

"Why?" Nydia asked. "It'll be great. Your lips will meet his and he'll look into your eyes and realize that, yes, it's you and only you that he's loved all along. Then he'll chuck that stupid girlfriend of his and go out with you and you'll get a two-page spread in *OK* magazine," she finished dreamily.

I shook my head. "He won't because I . . . I *can't* kiss him, Nydia. I have literally no idea *how* to kiss him! I haven't kissed *any* boy—*ever*—except for Danny in the school play and that was just on the cheek!" I bit my lip hard. "What am I going to do? I mean, they've given me this second chance to make it on the show and I really have to be brilliant, but how can I *act* at kissing him if I can't even kiss in real life? He'll hate me for making him look like a fool, and instead of mostly ignoring me like usual, he'll hate me forever and my life will be ruined."

Nydia looked puzzled. "Hang on a minute. You said you kissed that guy you met on holiday. You said so when we were all talking about kissing in the locker room last term, remember? So what's the problem, silly? You *have* done it before. You might be a bit rusty, but—"

"I was lying, you idiot," I told Nydia, maybe too abruptly, "so I didn't look so bad in front of Anne-Marie. She knows everything about kissing." I squirmed uncomfortably.

"Like how I looked bad, you mean," Nydia said, obviously feeling hurt that I hadn't told her the truth at the time. "So *that* was why you were so cagey about the details. You didn't have any."

I gave her my best apologetic look. "I'm sorry, Nyd," I told her. "But, well, it doesn't matter now, does it? The point is, I haven't kissed anyone ever and I don't know what to do!"

Nydia gave me the same look she gives her brothers when they've been especially irritating, and then she rolled her eyes and thought for a moment. "I know," she said, holding up her balled fist. "We can practice on the back of our hands!"

I looked at the back of my hand and made a "yuck" face. "How are the backs of our hands anything like Justin's lips?" I asked her. "Only kids try snogging the backs of their hands! Anyway, slobbering all over my own hand isn't going to give me any tips. It's just going to make me feel icky."

Nydia bit her lip and thought for a moment longer. "We could practice on the back of each other's hands?" she suggested mischievously.

I picked up one of her pillows and threw it at her. "Nydia! Don't be so disgusting!"

She laughed and flopped back against her pillows. "I know! What about when you have rehearsal?" she asked. "It doesn't matter if you're crap in the rehearsal, does it? After all, that's what they're for. You can rehearse your kiss, and by the time you come to shoot it for real, you'll be a pro."

I shook my head and sighed with exasperation.

"First of all, we never actually rehearse things like kisses; we leave them until filming so they look all spontaneous and fresh. Second of all, I have to be brilliant the *very first* time I kiss him, not after a hundred takes. He's not going to realize that he's really been in love with me all this time if I kiss like a cross between a vacuum cleaner and a fish!"

Nydia laughed so much she nearly fell off the bed. "You've never kissed *anyone*," she said once she got her breath back, "so how would you know *what* you kiss like?"

"It's a wild guess," I told her. She was still laughing. "Nydia, pull yourself together and think of something! I really need your help here!"

Finally, after several deep breaths, she calmed down and picked up her latest copy of *Elle Girl* for inspiration. "I know! How about we write in to the problem page here and ask them. I'll get some paper," she said, and before I could comment she had leaped off the bed and begun rummaging around under the mess that was her desk. I considered banging my head against her bedroom wall.

"Nydia! I haven't got time to write in to a problem page! And anyway, what with all the letters I get, my life practically *is* a problem page. I might as well write to myself."

Nydia stopped, mid-rummage, and looked at me. "There you go! That's a plan. Let's write to you and see what you say." She was still giggling. For some reason, she wasn't taking me completely seriously.

I buried my head in my hands and closed my eyes. "Nydia! I can't answer my own problems! If I could, I wouldn't be here in the first place practically having a panic attack over the most important moment of my life!"

Nydia sat back down on her bed and thought for a long moment. At least she'd stopped all the hysteria at my expense. "We need help," she said finally.

"I know, but I can't afford counseling," I said with a squeaky laugh.

This time Nydia didn't laugh. She leaned her head in her hands. "No, I mean we need someone who *really* knows what they're talking about. We need an expert consultant to teach you how to kiss."

I uncovered my face a little bit and looked at her. She was either a complete loony or a genius. I just wasn't sure which.

"An expert?" I asked her tentatively. "What are you talking about?"

Nydia shrugged. "Well, it's obvious when you think about it. We know totally nothing, so we need someone who knows totally everything—or *nearly* everything. We need someone who, say, knows everything about kissing."

My hands fell away from my face, my jaw dropped, and I shook my head in horror. She was officially a complete loony.

"Oh, no!" I spluttered. It took me a moment to let the full horror of what she was suggesting sink in. "No way. *No way!* We are *not* asking Anne-Marie Chance to tell me how to kiss Justin. She'll laugh her head off and then tell everyone. *You* might be able to handle the daily ritual humiliation, but I can't. I would truly die of embarrassment. They'd be able to make a documentary about me and put me on *National Geographic*: 'People Who Die of Ridicule: A Case Study.'"

Nydia pursed her lips and crossed her arms like she does when she thinks I'm being too dismissive of her ideas. "Ah, but we'd make it so she wouldn't be able to tell anyone," she said with a hint of menace, nodding at me as if I should be in on a secret that I had no idea about.

I shook my head. "You mean give her concrete stilettos and sink her in the Thames?" I wondered if my voice would ever stop squeaking and return to its normal pitch. On the other hand, if my career flopped I could always get a job doing voice-overs on *Charlie and Lola*.

"No, silly," Nydia said. "I mean we'll *bribe* her to keep quiet."

I reached into my pocket and pulled out three pounds and eighty-nine pence. "What, with this? Because this is all I have left out of my allowance, and it's only Wednesday. I don't think it'll cut much sway with a millionaire's daughter, do you?"

Nydia looked at the coins languishing in my palm. "What about your trust fund?" she said.

"No way, José," I replied. "I can't touch it. And anyway, Anne-Marie would never—"

"I know!" Nydia's eyes lit up, and I could see the

worst had happened. She'd had one of her mad plans again, the kind you can't get her to leave alone—the kind that always, *always* gets us into trouble. Only this time I had the feeling she was going to surpass herself.

"You said your mum is feeling guilty, right? And your dad too? Well, we'll find out what Anne-Marie wants—a mobile phone that can take photos or a PSP or something—and then get them to buy it for you and then we'll give it to her. Easy peasy."

I thought for a moment. "I don't know," I said. "They feel bad, but . . . oh, Nydia, this plan is ridiculous! It's never going to work. Anne-Marie won't help us, even for a cool mobile phone. And even if she would, my mum would never buy me one. You know what she's like about me being normal! Anyway, it doesn't seem very fair to Mum or Dad to rip them off like that."

Nydia took both my hands in hers. "Have they been fair to you?"

I shook my head, the bleak reality of what was waiting for me at home surging back for a second. All these plans, all this excitement over Justin: It was mad and silly, but it was better—*anything* was better—than thinking about *that*. I boxed up all thoughts of home and shoved them to the back of my mind.

"And besides," Nydia continued, "it would only be a

one-off. It's not as if you'd do it every week. You deserve to get something out of all this, Ruby, don't you?"

I nodded uncertainly. The only thing I really wanted was my family back the way it always had been. But I couldn't have that, so I'd just have to be tough. It was the only way to get through it.

"Have you got a better idea?" Nydia asked pointedly.

I shook my head.

"And do you want to be able to kiss Justin so well that he'll be blown away at what might be your only chance?"

My heart plummeted. But it was no good. I just couldn't do it.

"I can't," I said. "I just can't get Mum and Dad to buy me something to give to Anne-Marie. Even if I don't like them much at the moment. I'm sorry, Nyds."

Nydia squeezed my wrist and thought for a second longer. "Yes, you can," she said excitedly. "And you don't even need your mum and dad to do it. You've got the one thing that Anne-Marie wants more than anything else."

I looked confused. "What? A bra the size of a battleship?"

"No, silly. *Fame.* You've got fame and she hates that. If you told her that you could maybe help her get a part on the show . . ."

"But I can't," I protested. "I'm barely holding on to my own part."

Nydia shook her head quickly. "Yes, I know that, and you know that. But *she* doesn't, does she? She'd go for it. I bet she would. She dyed her hair orange to try to get the lead in *Annie*. If she'd do that, she'd do anything."

I nodded. "Maybe . . ." I said. Maybe I was overtired and overwrought, but Nydia's plan *did* have a mad kind of logic to it. And so what if it would mean lying to Anne-Marie? It's not as if she'd ever been anything but nasty to me.

Nydia was looking pleased with herself. "Well then," she said, "all we have to do is just call Anne-Marie and we'll see what she says, OK? There's no harm in that, is there? We won't say *exactly* why we need her help to start off with—just that we do. And if she turns us down flat, the worst she'll even be able to say around school is that we tried to suck up to her. If she agrees, then she'll have to keep her mouth shut or she won't get your help. It can't fail."

"It *can* fail," I said bleakly. "In fact, it probably *will* fail. But, oh well. Let's do it anyway."

Chapter Ten

"OK, I'll do it," Anne-Marie said.

Of course, it wasn't as easy as that. Nydia and I didn't just breeze up to Anne-Marie's posh mansion in Highgate the very next morning and sail past the security gate. We didn't just waltz into the marble-floored entrance hall, sweep up the curved staircase, pop into her suite of three rooms (including her own bathroom and dressing room), sit down on her balcony, and agree to it all over chilled Diet Coke.

First off, there was the phone call. Nydia decided that if we didn't put the wheels in motion right then and there we would chicken out the next day. She grabbed her mobile phone and called Anne-Marie's number without giving herself a chance to think. I don't know how or why she had Anne-Marie's number. Maybe it was left over from the time when we all first got mobiles, and it seemed more important to have a lot of numbers in your phone than whether the person was nice or not.

I had Menakshi's and Jade's numbers in my phone for about a week before I realized they were never going to call me and I was certainly never going to call them, and so I deleted them. Nydia, on the other hand, still harbored these fantasies that we were living in a real-life teen movie where the lame kids like us eventually become cool and everybody is friends in the end. That's the kind of optimistic person she is.

Anyway, I thought Anne-Marie would see it was Nydia calling and just ignore the call without even picking up, but it looked like she must have deleted Nydia's number, because she answered. I pressed my ear to the other side of the phone to hear the conversation. My heart was thundering in my chest.

"Hi-iiii!" Anne-Marie sang into the phone.

"Hi, Anne-Marie. How are you?" Nydia said.

"Fine, fine. *Who* are you?" Anne-Marie replied archly.

"It's Nydia, um, from school. Listen I was just wondering—"

"Nydia?" Anne-Marie was clearly shocked. "How did you get my number?"

"You gave it to me," Nydia said, looking slightly hurt. "Anyway—"

"I don't remember giving it to *you*. Anyway, whatever it is, no. No, I do not want to come to one of your lame sleepovers, or join in on one of your stupid film projects, or even walk on the same side of the street as you. OK?"

Nydia looked at me and rolled her eyes. I shook my head, drawing my forefinger sharply across my throat in what I hoped was the universal sign for "Cut!"

But Nydia ignored me. "Hang on," she said quickly. "Just listen for a minute. It won't cost you anything to listen—and it could be to your advantage." She tried to be all mysterious but instead sounded like she had a nasty cold.

Anne-Marie nearly choked on her own laughter. "I'm listening because, luckily for you, I'm alone and bored and could do with a good laugh. But hurry up." I pictured her tapping her pink nails impatiently.

"Well," Nydia took a deep breath, "Ruby and I need your help. We need you to coach Ruby with a scene that's coming up on *Kensington Heights*. Sort of like Method acting. It's an area where Ruby hasn't had much experience and, well, we thought you could maybe offer your advice? Because you're *such* a good actress, after all."

There was a pause, and I imagined the expression on Anne-Marie's face was somewhere between disbelieving hysteria and horror. After all, I more or less felt like that, and I wasn't even *her*.

"Me? Coach Little Miss I'm-So-Brilliant-and-Famous?" Anne-Marie barked out a harsh laugh. "No way. If she'd ever wanted any help from me she should have gotten off her high horse years ago and stopped acting so snotty about being on TV. She's got everything! She doesn't need me! And even if she did, I certainly wouldn't help her. I mean, she's so high and mighty that she can't even ring and ask me herself; she has to get her little servant to do it."

My jaw dropped and I looked at Nydia. Anne-Marie calling *me* snooty? *Me* stuck-up? I tried to grab the phone from Nydia to tell Anne-Marie exactly what I thought of her, but she tussled it out of my hands, held me at arm's length, and glared at me until I signaled that I would listen quietly again.

"I know," Nydia said with surprising calm. "You're right. She *can* come across as a snob sometimes, but it's basically only to cover up her many insecurities. She didn't phone you tonight because, well, I haven't told her I'm calling you. I wanted to see if you'd help us before I raised her hopes. She really does respect you, Anne-Marie. More than you know. She actually looks up to you."

I stuck my finger down my throat and mimed vomiting onto the floor.

Nydia motioned for me to shush. "And just think, if you help Ruby now, maybe she'll be able to get you some introductions on the show like she did for Danny Harvey—"

"*Danny's* got a part on *Kensington Heights*?" Anne-Marie exclaimed. "I *knew* she fancied him; it was so obvious! God, how sick is that, trying to buy a boyfriend? If it wasn't for the fact you've got no other friends and no one else would even talk to you, I'd tell you to drop her, Nydia."

Nydia winced as if Anne-Marie had slapped her face and, taking a deep breath, put on her stage smile.

I felt horrible. She was only putting herself through all of this for me. She really was the world's best friend.

"No! No, she doesn't fancy Danny. Not at all," Nydia exclaimed. "They just talked a bit during the school play last year and she decided to help him out. She could help you out too—get you on the set and introduce you to a few important people." She paused for a moment to let the idea sink in before adding, "Apparently they're looking for a new teenager . . ."

Anne-Marie was silent again for what seemed like forever.

"How do I know you're not just feeding me a pack of lies?" she said, her voice as cold as ice.

Nydia and I exchanged looks. That was a tricky one because, after all, that's exactly what we were doing.

Nydia steeled herself. "Because we need you to help us," she said evenly, looking at me and crossing her fingers. "And because you can trust us."

"Trust you two? The original stupid twins?" Anne-Marie snorted, sounding like a pig. "As if!"

"OK, then," Nydia said quickly. "Fine. We'll drop it. But when you see someone else with the part, don't go blaming us."

Anne-Marie sighed. "No, no . . . hang on a minute. Tell me exactly what I'd have to do and I'll think about it."

"Er, we can't tell you exactly how you're helping us until we meet you tomorrow, and you must *never* tell anyone *anything* about this. Ruby will arrange for you to get on the set and meet all the right people, but that will only happen after completion of the agreement. So what do you say? Will you do it?" Nydia held my hand so tightly the tips of my fingers went white.

"You know, Nydia, it's lucky for you that you know Ruby, isn't it? Otherwise your fat little life would be really boring." Nydia flinched again, and I squeezed her fingers back. "You'd better not be winding me up. If I find out this is one of your stupid little scams, I swear I'll make you pay."

Nydia looked at me and winked. "It's not a scam. Ruby can make it happen. *She's* on the telly, remember?" Nydia said it in such a way as to remind Anne-Marie that she wasn't on the telly, never had been, and hadn't even done an ad in a year.

There was a long and agonizing silence.

"OK, I'll do it," Anne-Marie said. So we arranged to go to her place in the morning and sort it all out then. Just like that.

"You heard her," I said later—after we'd calmed down and stopped jumping on the bed like idiots. "She's totally going to kill us. At least now she just ignores us. After this she's going to . . . she's going to . . . well, *kill* us."

Nydia smiled and gave me a hug. "Relax, Ruby. It'll be fine. We'll worry about that after we've got your kiss out of the way. She'll probably just forget about it anyway."

I shook my head in disbelief. "Yeah, right!" I exclaimed. All my excitement was suddenly gone. I felt sick again. "You shouldn't have told her that I helped Danny. I didn't even know he was going to be on the show until today! I mean, I just very nearly got sacked myself. The last thing I have is any influence."

"I know," Nydia said. "But I had to have a way in with her. It's the only thing she understands."

I nodded. "And what about her calling me stuck-up? Imagine that!"

"Imagine," Nydia agreed.

Nydia's dad took me home just before nine thirty. The house was quiet except for the murmur of the TV in the living room, so I stood in the hallway for a few seconds, waiting for Mum to call out to me. When she didn't, I peeked around the door. She was asleep in the chair with a glass of red wine in her hand. I stood there for a moment and wondered what to do. Eventually I tiptoed in and carefully lifted the glass out of her hand. It was filled to the brim, and the open bottle on the coffee table was still half full, so at least she hadn't got herself drunk like Angel's mum did in the show.

I set the glass down on the table and looked at her. Her mouth was open and her eyes were closed tightly, her brows furrowed as if she were dreaming in frowns. I took a pen from the desk and wrote on the back of an envelope, "I'm back, Ruby xoxo," and rested it on her knees. Then I went to bed.

I don't know what the time was, but I'd been asleep for a while when I heard her come into my room, just like she used to when I was a kid. I kept my eyes closed and my breathing steady as she sat on the edge of my bed. She brushed the hair off my face and kissed my cheek.

"Sleep well, my baby," she whispered. "I love you."

I lay very still as she left the room, pretending to be asleep, but it was a long time before I was.

29 Windhouse Street
Brighton
Sussex

Dear Angel,

Last year your mum and dad split up for a while and you were really sad. Do you remember when they had a big custody battle over you and you thought that you were going to have to choose between them? Then you all got trapped in that lift as it hung by a single wire for two episodes and you realized that you all loved each other more than anything and they called off the divorce.

So I know you will understand how I feel,

Angel. My mum and dad have split up too. My mum has got a new boyfriend; she got him before she split up with Dad and now Dad is very angry. He doesn't live at home now and Mum won't let him near the house. She says she'll get a restraining order if he even tries to talk to me or my little brother, Josh. He's not even allowed to pick us up from school. Mum says that Dad is a bad person and that he has never really loved us. Dad told me Mum doesn't care about anything or anyone except herself and that we should come and live with him. We have to see a social worker soon and tell her what we think.

The thing is, Angel, I know they still love each other really—just like your mum and dad. How can I make them see it? We don't live near any tall buildings with lifts, and anyway Mum won't go in one ever since she saw that episode of *Kensington Heights.*

Thank you for listening,
Naomi Torrence

Chapter Eleven

I looked at Naomi's letter for a long time after it arrived this morning with the rest of the post from the studio. I couldn't think of anything to say. How could I tell her that Angel's mum and dad only got back together because Trudy had written it that way—not because of anything that might happen to a real girl like Naomi or a real girl like me. I should be glad, I suppose, that my mum and dad haven't said or done the things that Naomi's mum and dad have. But I'm not.

I read the letter again, and part of me wanted to write back and tell her I *did* know exactly how she felt. I did know because it was happening to me too, and it didn't matter if it happened to one in three families or one in three billion, because when it happens to you it feels like the worst thing in the world. But somehow I couldn't do it. I couldn't write anything to Naomi, and my usual pep talk and leaflet for ChildLine seemed pointless.

For the first time I thought about what *I* would do if someone told me to talk to a teacher, or my mum, or a stranger on the end of the phone—even a very nice one. I didn't know if I'd be able to take that advice. To say the words—to really say out loud the things that are worrying you—is hard, maybe too hard. Maybe it's best just to pretend they aren't there and get on with things. But I can't write that to Naomi; she needs someone to tell her that everything is going to be OK one day. I don't know if it is anymore though, not for her or for me.

So I folded the letter up and tucked it into my pillowcase (which is where I plan to put the love letters that Justin will write me one day), and I pulled out my scripts for the next four shows. Everest pushed open my bedroom door with his nose and looked at me before lumbering up to my bed. I reached down and helped him up beside me, pulling the scripts he was lying on out from under his tummy.

I looked at them in their pale yellow covers, with the *Kensington Heights* logo swirled across the little window that showed the episode number and title. Normally, I'd take it downstairs and Mum would go through it with me and highlight my lines, and we'd give them a general read-through so I knew how Angel was supposed to be thinking and feeling, and then I'd sort of learn them. I say "sort of" because it's not like a play where you always have to get it right all the time. I mean, you *do* have to get it right, but you can improvise too—make up your own way of saying the line, as long as when we get to the end of the scene everyone is happy. Our schedule is too tight to learn them all by heart. But when Mum brought my tea in this morning her eyes were red and her nose looked swollen; she'd been crying again. I didn't want her to feel like she had to hide it from me so I thought I should stay out of her way.

Anyway, on the third script there was a bright pink Post-it note with Trudy's handwriting crawling over it in fat blue marker pen. "Read this scene first! It's so fab!" I picked up the script and turned to the page she'd marked. I knew exactly which scene it was before I read it, but that didn't stop my heart from pounding like a drum and my hands from shaking as I read the words.

KENSINGTON HEIGHTS
SERIES NINE, EPISODE FOURTEEN
"FIRST LOVE FOREVER"
WRITTEN BY: *TRUDY SIMMONS*

<u>SCENE THIRTY-TWO</u>

<u>EXT. GARDEN: MOONLIGHT</u>

ANGEL stands alone in CASPIAN's garden, having rushed out of the party. She looks up at the moon, tears brimming in her eyes. She is mortified that JULIA has told CASPIAN about her crush on him. She knows that everyone will be laughing at her. CASPIAN enters the garden.

                    CASPIAN
Angel?

CASPIAN rests his hand on ANGEL'S shoulder, making her jump. ANGEL turns and looks up at him.

CASPIAN

Don't stay out here on your own. Come
inside. It's almost time for the cake.

ANGEL

Cake? That's all you think of me, isn't
it? You think I'm some silly little
girl who likes cake!

ANGEL is struggling to hold back her
tears. CASPIAN brushes her hair away
from her face and shakes his head.

CASPIAN

Look, Julia did tell me what you said
to her—about liking me, I mean, and
wishing that it could be me who gives
you your first kiss. I don't know why
you told her; you must have known she
would tell. She's probably just jealous. She's always catty when she's
jealous.

ANGEL turns away from him and buries
her head in her hands.

ANGEL

Oh, please! Just leave me alone. I know you hate me. It's fine! You don't have to pretend to be nice to me. Just go inside back to Julia!

CASPIAN holds ANGEL gently by the shoulder and turns her back to face him.

CASPIAN

But I don't hate you! I, well, these last few weeks, the way you've dealt with being a hostage in that armed robbery and the way you've done your hair . . . it's made me see you differently. I can see you're growing up, Angel, into a really beautiful woman.

ANGEL

You can?

CASPIAN

Yes, I can. The thing is, Angel—since I'm almost sixteen and you aren't even

fourteen—I just think that now isn't
the right time for you and me. I think
we've all got a bit of growing up to do
first, don't you? You are an amazing
person, but you've got all the time in
the world. You don't need to rush something like falling in love.

                    ANGEL

I didn't rush into it. It just happened. (Pauses.) Caspian? Do you think
that, maybe one day you might . . . like
me too?

CASPIAN laughs gently and cups ANGEL'S
face in his hands.

                   CASPIAN

I like you now, Angel. I always will.
And even if I can't give you more than
that, I don't see why I can't make at
least one of your wishes come true.

Close-up on pair. ANGEL looks up into
CASPIAN'S eyes and he moves to kiss
her. She closes her eyes and he gently,

softly, tenderly, sweetly kisses her on
the lips. He pulls back. Her eyes are
still closed.

CASPIAN
(Smiling at ANGEL, seeing the beautiful
woman she will become.) Now, will you
come inside and have some cake?

ANGEL opens her eyes and nods, too happy
to speak. CASPIAN goes inside; after a
moment of looking up at the stars,
ANGEL follows him. She senses that this
is the beginning of a new phase in her
life. She is walking on air.

For a second I *was* walking on air. For one second I
could smell the scent of the evening flowers, feel the
silver of the moonlight on my skin and the brush of
Justin's warm lips against mine . . .

And then I had a panic attack. I have to admit I'd
imagined over and over again what Justin's lips might
feel like: soft (but not too soft) and warm. But what
did *mine* feel like? Maybe *my* lips were rubbery and
damp, or cold and clammy! And did I have to pucker
up and purse them? Or just keep them still? Maybe I

should even open my lips like they did in the movies.

Panic-stricken, I looked at the clock. I'd promised Nydia I would meet her outside Anne-Marie's house at ten A.M. and that I wouldn't make her wait or go in on her own. But what with Naomi's letter and the script, I'd lost track of time. I only had fifteen minutes to get there—and it was a thirty-minute bus ride away.

I leaped out of bed and pulled my jeans off the back of the chair, getting dressed as quickly as possible. I should have had a shower and brushed my hair, but I didn't have time. I ran downstairs and past the kitchen, where my mum was making tea.

"I'm just going to meet Nydia and her mum and I'm late, OK? I'll be back by lunch." I rushed for the front door, hoping the inevitable wouldn't happen.

Inevitably, it did.

"Hang on a minute!"

I stopped in my tracks and looked at Mum. She had washed her face and, although she looked tired, you almost couldn't tell that she'd been crying. She smiled at me.

"Where are you going, Ruby? It's just that I thought we could both go shopping. We haven't been for ages, have we? We could get you some new clothes. Nydia could come too, if you like, and we could all go to lunch."

I stared at her and found myself wondering if she would buy me a new phone, since she was feeling guilty at the moment. But then I felt terrible. Poor Mum thought she was being nice to me—and she *was* being really nice to me. She thought that if she took me out, then maybe I'd be nice to her. And all I could think about was getting new stuff that she'd never normally buy me. But it's like I said before, I just couldn't think about the things Mum wanted me to think about right now. I had to get away from all of that: from her crying, and from Dad not being in the kitchen, ironing his shirt and making his own words up to the songs on the radio. My chest felt hollow and empty.

"I'm sorry, Mum, I can't today," I said. "Nydia and I and this other girl from school . . . we're rehearsing this play and I need to go. But maybe on my next day off? I'd like that." I bit my lip and looked at my feet. Somehow I'd made it sound as if I were lying.

"That's OK." Mum was still smiling, but I could see that she had to work really hard to keep the corners of her mouth pointing upward. "It's just that . . . well . . . you're not bottling everything up, are you, darling?"

I stared hard at the toe of my shoe. Of course I'm bottling everything up. Why would anybody want to un-bottle what I'm feeling and pour it all over the place, making a great big mess? But I didn't say that out loud, because the last thing I wanted was for her to *make* me talk about it—or worse, to get it into her head that I needed a counselor, like Jade Caruso's parents did when she was caught shoplifting in New Look. (It wasn't the shoplifting that had shocked them; it was the fact that she'd chosen New Look instead of some designer place. At least, that's what Nydia and I thought.) I'd overheard Jade talking about it once. She said it was the most embarrassing and humiliating moment of her life and that, in the end, she'd had to cry and pretend to be miserable just so they'd let her out of the house on her own again.

"I'm not bottling it up, Mum, I'm just . . . I'm OK. Really." I gave her my best smile, hoping to reassure her.

"Your dad called last night," she said. "He's going to come over later and take you out for pizza."

My shoulders slumped. *"Pizza,"* I said. "He never used to take me out for pizza on my own. I don't want to go out for pizza with just him. Everyone will look at us and they'll know, won't they? They'll know I have to go out for pizza with my dad because he doesn't live at home anymore."

My mum crossed the hallway and gave me a big

hug, which was probably what she'd wanted to do all along.

"I know, but your dad is trying, Ruby. And he misses you." She squeezed me hard. "Besides, the only reason people will look at you is because you're the girl from the telly. People's parents split up all the time. You're not the only girl this has happened to, you know."

I drew back and looked at her. "I'm the only girl it's happened to who's me!" I said. I didn't want to see Dad. Every time I thought about seeing him, the memory of me asking him to stay and him saying no almost came out again until I pushed it really tightly back inside my head. But if I didn't go, then I knew Mum would feel even more worried and guilty than she already did. *Mum* was at least trying to be nice to me. *Dad*, on the other hand, deserved everything he got.

"OK," I said. "OK, I'll go for *pizza*." I spat out the word like an old piece of chewing gum. Mum ruffled my hair. Since she was feeling a bit low, I didn't complain like I usually do.

"Things are hard right now, Rube," she said with a sad smile. "But they'll get better, I promise. Off you go."

I hesitated for a second longer, but then thought of

Nydia, who was probably already at Anne-Marie's house and fuming at me for being late.

"Bye, then," I said, kissing her quickly on the cheek.

I ran all the way to the bus stop, but I just missed one and the next bus took twenty minutes to come. I tried to call Nydia, but all I got was her voice mail.

Nydia was going to kill me.

Chapter Twelve

Anne-Marie's house was exactly like I described—complete with the security gate, not to mention marble pillars and a nice Spanish housekeeper who answered the door when I (finally) got to it. It was a huge door too, about the size of four normal doors all glued together. I knew there were houses like this in Highgate, but I hadn't actually been to one. In fact, I hadn't even been *past* one, because they were always behind lots of trees set far back from the road.

"Come this way, miss," the housekeeper said. "Your friend is already here. She is in the garden with Anne-Marie."

If Anne-Marie had come to my house, it would

have taken her about thirty seconds to get from my front door to the back garden. But it seemed to take us forever going through room after huge room. Eventually we came out onto a terrace, and the housekeeper pointed me in the direction of a swimming pool. Not just a paddling pool but an *actual* swimming pool. I said to Mum once a couple of years ago that I wouldn't mind if we used my money from the show to buy a bigger house—maybe even one with a pool. But Mum had just laughed and asked exactly how much did I think I earned anyway and, besides, she wanted me to have a normal family life in a normal family house and grow up to be a normal, well-adjusted adult, etc. Well, so much for that plan.

I could see Anne-Marie reclining on a sunlounger in a pink bikini and matching sarong. Nydia was perched on the edge of another, wriggling uncomfortably under the heat of the sun and the glare that Anne-Marie was probably giving her from underneath her sunglasses. Poor Nydia. I shouldn't have let her go through this alone.

"Would you like a drink?" the housekeeper asked me. "I'll bring you one."

"Oh, yes please," I said gratefully. I had run all the way here from the bus and I was hot and sticky. "And could my friend have another one too, please?"

The housekeeper nodded. "You're a very nice girl with nice manners—unlike her friends. Right little madams, most of them." She threw a look at Anne-Marie. "Although, with my little Annie, her bark is much worse than her bite, trust me!" Then, before turning back to the house, she said, "I love your show, never miss it."

I took a deep breath and walked down the steps of the terrace where Anne-Marie and Nydia sat.

"Hi!" I said, sitting next to Nydia.

"I waited for you for ages," she said sulkily under her breath. "And then I thought I'd better go in, otherwise she'd think we weren't coming and she'd go shopping or something." She looked glumly at Anne-Marie, and I tried to imagine the torture she'd been going through, waiting for me.

"I'm sorry I'm late," I said to Anne-Marie. "It's just that my scripts came and—"

"Blah, blah, blah," Anne-Marie interrupted me, flapping her hands like a duck's beak. "I'm so important, yak, yak, yak, who cares about anybody else." She rolled her eyes. "You can't pull your prima-donna stunts here, OK? If you want my help, you turn up when you say you're going to turn up. I have plans later, you know. I do actually have a life. Now, tell me what this scene is that you're too stupid to be able to act and let's get on with it."

I tried to smile, but suddenly the thought of going through with this plan seemed more ridiculous than ever. All I could think was that I needed to escape somehow. I needed to get us out of there before Nydia told her the whole story.

"Your house is amazing," I said, hoping to stall her with some small talk while I thought of a way to escape. "Where are your parents?"

Anne-Marie looked bored. "Dad's in LA. Again. Mum's in Milan until next week, and then she's going to Tokyo. My brother, Chris, is in Ladbroke Grove staying at his girlfriend's place, as usual."

I frowned. "So you're living here in this enormous house on your own?" I asked, not sure if that was really great or really terrible. "Is that even legal at our age?"

"No, idiot. I'm not on my own. Pilar, the housekeeper, lives here too. And the man who does the gardening comes in every day. Chris is *supposed* to be here, but he never is. It's no big deal," she said breezily, her eyes masked by her shades.

"But . . . aren't you lonely?" I asked her.

She pushed up her sunglasses and shook her head. For a moment she looked sort of smaller and younger— more like an average thirteen-year-old girl instead of a hard-as-nails vixen. Then she opened her mouth.

"Of course I'm not *lonely*! I've got hundreds of friends, and a boyfriend who's coming over later. You and sad sack here are the lonely ones. Anyway, I don't mind. It means I can do what I like." She sat up and looked directly at me. "It means I can have people like you over with no one having to know about it. Now, stop trying to stall and tell me what it is you want. Otherwise I'll be so bored you'll have to leave before I slip into a coma."

And then I knew it was too late. I wasn't getting out of this plan.

So we told her. Well, actually, Nydia told her. First Anne-Marie looked horrified, then delighted, and then she just laughed and laughed and laughed until she went pink from her ears down. Either that or she hadn't put any sunblock on.

"Oh my God!" she shrieked as she reached for her phone. "Just wait until Jade hears about this!"

Nydia reached out her hand in a stopping motion. "Hang on. Remember what we agreed," she said, sounding quite cross for her, but not cross enough to stop Anne-Marie.

"That was before I knew what you wanted me to do. You want *me* to teach *her* how to kiss. Me? You must think I'm crazy. I always thought you two were weird. You're probably lesbians." She keyed in Jade's number and held the phone to her ear. "This is brilliant," she said as she waited for Jade to pick up.

I looked at Nydia, wide-eyed with panic, waiting for her to come up with one of her plans. She didn't. She just sat there as if she were frozen solid, even under the heat of the sun.

"OK," I said, desperately trying to act as if I didn't care. "OK, fine. I'll just cancel the meeting I made for you next week with our producer, Liz Hornby, then."

Anne-Marie's laugh froze on her face.

"Oh, hi, Jade. Yeah, yeah, I do, but listen, I'll call you back, OK? Something's just come up." She put her phone down. "You've already set up a meeting with Liz Hornby?" she said, looking at me.

I am an actress, so, really, I should be very good at lying. After all, everything I do on-screen is basically me trying to convince people I'm someone I'm not. But when it comes to *actual* lying—off set and in the real world—I'm terrible. I can't look at the person I'm lying to and my voice goes all silly and small.

"Er, yes," I said, trying to sound normal. "It's all been arranged, but it can easily be unarranged. There's a new part coming up, but . . ."

Just at that moment, Pilar arrived with two drinks. Nydia and I both took ours and drank them down in one gulp.

"But it's ridiculous! How can I teach you to kiss?" Anne-Marie said. "It's not something you *teach*. It's something you sort of just *learn*."

I sighed. "I can't just learn it, Anne-Marie. I haven't got time to learn it *or* anyone to learn it with. It's supposed to be my first kiss, and I want my first kiss to be with Justin. It's got to be perfect."

Anne-Marie grinned like the Cheshire Cat from *Alice in Wonderland*. "You fancy Justin de Souza, don't you? Justin, the star of the show, the teen hunk! You fancy him and you seriously think that he might like you! You! Poor guy—has he read the script yet? He'll probably resign when he does and then you won't have to worry anymore."

I stood up and looked at Nydia. "This is pointless," I said. "Let's just go." Nydia stood up too, but Anne-Marie waved for her to sit back down . She did with a *plonk*.

"Hang on," Anne-Marie said. "Kissing scenes are easy, really. You don't even have to worry about tongue. You just need to get the mood right; get your nose in the right place and you'll be fine. And as you've *so* got the hots for Justin, you'll have no problem. You just need someone to practice on. I'll arrange it, OK? If you stick to your side of the agreement, that is."

I looked uncertainly at Nydia. "OK, but when? I'm

on the set tomorrow and I got the new scripts today with the kissing scene in them. The read-through will be on Monday and we'll start shooting it Thursday."

Anne-Marie thought for a moment.

"Tomorrow evening. *Here*. No one will be here anyway."

"OK," Nydia and I said together.

Nydia picked up her bag. "Listen, Anne-Marie, thanks a lot for doing this . . ." she began.

"Don't thank *me*. You know why I'm doing it. I must be the only girl in the world whose father is a movie producer and won't pull any strings to get her parts. He says if I want respect in the business, I have to make my own way. Well, I'm making my own way. I'm pulling your strings and that's all, so don't start getting all excited and thinking we'll be friends. We won't. Ever." She picked up a magazine from under her chair and opened it. "You can go now. I'll see you tomorrow."

We walked through the house and down the long drive, back to the real world of traffic fumes and noise.

"Well, that was hideous," I said. "I'm so sorry I was late." Nydia scowled at me. "I'm sorry, Nydia! I wouldn't have been, honest, but Mum wanted to 'talk' to me and I couldn't just go, could I? Not with her and Dad . . . you know."

Nydia sighed. "I know," she said. "But she's so

horrible to me, Ruby. She's even more horrible to me than she is to you. I just don't get why; I really don't. What have I ever done to make her hate me so much? She makes me feel like I'm not even a person. Like I don't even have feelings that count."

I put an arm around Nydia's shoulder and we bump-walked together along the road. "She treats you like that because that's how she feels about herself," I said, using a line I'd thought of for one of my problem-letter replies. "Nydia, you're not only a person, you're the best person in the whole world. A million times better than Anne-Marie! You're always there for me. And I know how horrible it was for you sucking up to her today, but you know I'd always do the same for you, don't you?"

"Yeah, I do," Nydia said. "Although I never get myself into those situations. The worst thing I've got myself into was detention for two weeks." She grinned at me and giggled. "Poor Anne-Marie. It must be so hard being thin and blonde with those big blue eyes and all that money. Poor her."

"Yes, poor her," I said. "Poor little Anne-Marie." Then I remembered what I'd promised her. "She's going to be really, really *angry* Anne-Marie pretty soon."

"What do you mean?" Nydia asked.

"When she finds out I haven't arranged any meeting with Liz. That never in millions of years could I arrange any meetings for anyone. I'm only a kid! She must think I'm miles more important than I am. That's really going to hack her off when she finds out."

Nydia giggled even more, and we both laughed our way to the bus stop until I remembered something else Anne-Marie had said.

"Hang on a minute. What did she mean when she said she would get someone for me to practice on?"

Chapter Thirteen

S o, what are you having then, kiddo?" Dad said.

Kiddo? He had never called me kiddo before in my whole life. I stared at him from around the edge of my menu. He was wearing this stupid bright red shirt and a stupid new leather jacket. There was something else funny going on. I squinted at him and realized he'd put gel in his hair and made it all spiky, even around the bits where you could see the pink of his scalp. If it wasn't so sad, it'd be funny. I wondered if he'd gotten himself a girlfriend.

"Your hair looks stupid like that," I said. "I'll have the marinara. A large one."

"All to yourself?" Dad attempted to joke. "You'll burst!"

"Are you saying I'm fat?" I asked without cracking a smile.

"What? No! Ruby, you're perfect. I'm glad you don't worry about what you eat. Too many girls do, especially girls in your industry. It's not worth it."

I rolled my eyes.

"I know that, Dad. I'm not a total moron." I looked around the restaurant. It was one of our favorite places; we'd been coming here since I was really little. All the staff knew us, and most of the time the other regulars either didn't recognize me or simply ignored me. But tonight there was a big family party in the corner who kept looking over at me and nudging one another. I tried not to look at them.

"Hi, Ruby. Hi, Mr. Parker. How's it going?" Cassie stopped at our table, her pen and order pad poised. "No Mrs. Parker tonight?"

My dad opened his mouth, but I stepped in before he could say anything.

"No, no. Mum's ill. Got the flu—terrible flu—had to stay in bed, and we can't cook so we came out to eat. She's really, *really* ill. But not so ill that it would be mean to leave her on her own or anything. Just too ill to cook."

Cassie looked concerned. "Poor Mrs. Parker. I know—I'll get some tiramisu for you to take away for her. That'll make her feel better. What do you reckon, Ruby?"

I nodded gratefully. Cassie took our orders and headed back to the kitchen, past the family who kept looking at me. Dad smiled at me. It was a new kind of smile—one he'd only got since he'd left—the sort of smile TV presenters give you when they're telling you how much they love your work. It was a fake smile.

"Ruby," he said brightly. "Darling, I know this is hard for you—I realize that—but, well, there's no point in pretending that it hasn't happened. People have to know sometime."

"Why?" I asked him in a low whisper. I nodded in the direction of the family who kept looking at me. "Those people over there, they recognize me from the telly. Do they *have* to know that my parents are splitting up? How do you think that feels, Dad? Or Cassie, who's known us since I only ate toast and butter here. Does she have to know? Does she have to know that my life's been ripped apart by *you*? I don't think so. I don't think anyone *has* to know."

Dad rubbed his hand across his chin and thought for a moment, as if he were trying to find a magic spell that would suddenly make everything all right.

"Darling, you mustn't think that this is happening *because* of you. I love you. Never forget that."

I forced myself not to laugh out loud. "You don't love me enough to stay at home," I snapped at him. "You don't love me enough to try to work things out with Mum." I slammed down my glass. "Do you?"

I could tell he was shocked. Before all this, it had always been him and me. Always us two joking around, teasing Mum or making her cross. Always him I went to when Mum said no. Always him who said yes—until Mum overruled him. He must have thought I'd be on his side in all this. He thought wrong.

"Ruby, you have to see this isn't about you. It isn't about how much I love you. It's about me and your mum being happy. We're not happy together and things have gone too far now for us to be happy together again. There's no way we could get back together. Your mum accepts that; she understands it. You have to try, too."

Just at that moment Cassie arrived and set down our pizzas. "Anyone for parmesan or ground pepper?" she asked us cheerfully.

"No, thanks," my dad said.

Cassie looked at us both. She must have known that something was up, because normally whenever we went there we made a joke about how much extra cheese I like on my pizza. She must have seen the red blotches blossoming on my cheeks and maybe the tears that were edging their way out of my eyes, because she didn't say anything more. She didn't make a joke or ask me about the show; she just turned and went.

I bit my lip hard and took a deep breath.

"Mum might tell you she's fine, Dad, but she isn't. She cries all the time. Her eyes are red all the time. She's only accepted it because you aren't giving her a choice."

I picked up my fork and stabbed it angrily into a piece of pizza. Dad shifted uncomfortably in his chair.

"Ruby, that's not true. Your mum and I agreed. And we also agreed that whatever happens we'll make sure that you don't—"

"Is it because you've got a new girlfriend?" I asked him. It was as if I'd just thought of it, but somehow I'd kept the question hidden even from myself until that moment, when it just came out without me telling it to.

"I . . . er . . . well, no, not in the sense you mean."

It was like I'd been punched in the stomach. I didn't know *what* I'd expected, but I hadn't expected him to admit to it. I hadn't expected it to be true. I couldn't believe that Dad could love someone else apart from me and Mum—someone else *instead* of us.

"You have? You've got a girlfriend?" I asked in disbelief. My voice rose above the murmur of the restaurant and the watching family all turned and stared at us.

"No. No!" Dad said quickly. And then, choosing his words carefully, he added, "There is . . . someone. But she's a friend and that's all. Nothing has happened, Ruby. We haven't even been on a date. We're just friends. But I do enjoy her company. One day, when things have settled down a bit, maybe then, but we'll see."

Until then, I hadn't really believed he was gone. Until then, I thought he'd come around; that eventually he'd hate how angry and hurt I was, and he'd get lonely and realize he missed us and just come home. But in that moment, I realized he was planning a future in which he was more than Mum's husband and more than my dad. He was planning a future without either of us in it.

"I want to go home," I said with a small, tight voice.

"But we haven't . . ." Dad gestured at my barely touched pizza.

"Please, Dad. I'm tired and I feel sick and I've got work in the morning. Please."

Dad ran his fingers through his stupid spiky hair and suddenly he looked very tired and older than normal. He shrugged and left some money on the table to pay the bill.

"I'm sorry, Ruby. I just can't seem to get things right at the moment," he said. "Come on, then."

I followed him out, keeping my eyes down as we threaded through the tables of other customers.

"Excuse me?" someone called out. My dad kept walking, but I stopped in my tracks. A girl from the corner table had reached her hand out to get my attention. I turned and made myself smile.

"I'm sorry to bother you, but you're Angel, aren't you? From *Kensington Heights*?"

I nodded. "That's me!" I said as cheerfully as I could.

"We love *Kensington Heights*, don't we, Mum?"

The girl's mother nodded. "Never miss it. Can't wait for next week!" She winked at her daughter. "It's Cheryl's birthday tonight. Well, her actual birthday's not till Saturday, but her dad's got her this weekend, so we thought we'd go out tonight."

"Happy birthday, Cheryl," I said with some effort.

"Um, do you, would you mind . . ." Cheryl asked nervously. "Would you give me your autograph, since it's my birthday? I'm thirteen, like you!"

I smiled, nodded, and signed the piece of paper she handed me, wishing her many happy returns.

"There you go," I said.

"I love Angel the best," Cheryl said. "She's the one you really believe in. All those other characters, they're just not real. But you—you're really real."

"Thanks," I managed to say. "All the best, then!" I turned on my heel and almost ran outside onto the street where Dad was waiting in his car. I could feel the tears starting to come again.

"Ruby," Dad said when I got in, "none of this was ever meant to hurt you. None of it."

I looked at him and wiped my tears away with my hands. "But it *does* hurt me, Dad," I told him. "It hurts me more than anything."

After we got back, Mum and Dad stood for a long time in the hallway, talking in low voices. Before tonight I'd have hoped they were trying to work things out—for my sake. But now I realized that really wasn't going to happen. However they worked things out, it wouldn't involve us getting back to the way we were. Dad hadn't really wanted to talk about his so-called friend, but somehow I knew from the moment he mentioned her, nothing would be the same again.

When Dad had gone, Mum brought me cheese toasties and a mug of hot chocolate with whipped cream.

"He *is* trying," she said as she sat down next to me on the sofa, tucking her legs up underneath her. I looked at her sideways. I wasn't sure if I should tell her about what Dad had told me or not. I didn't want to upset her. But I decided that she would want to know, that she'd hate for me to keep something from her.

"Mum? Did he tell you about his . . . friend?" I asked uncertainly.

Mum stretched her mouth into a thin, unhappy smile. "I know who she is, yes," she said. She put an arm around me and sat close to me as I picked at my cheese toasty. "Look, Ruby, it hurts. It hurts a lot to think about your dad being with someone else. I suppose that's why I've been crying so much. But it's not because I want your dad back. It's because I'm sad when I think about how happy we were when we started out. I'm sorry we couldn't keep it that way, but your dad and I don't make each other happy anymore. I'm not saying we don't still love each other in a way—just not in the way we used to. He thinks he might find that kind of love with another person. That's hard to understand, I know, especially when you've been so used to things being one way for such a long time. But I *do* understand it. I'm not the victim in this, Ruby, so don't make your dad the bad guy just because you need someone to blame. He loves you very, very much."

I slurped my hot chocolate. "He won't love me when he's got loads of new kids," I said. "He'll probably just forget about me then."

Mum shook her head and kissed the top of mine. "He won't, Ruby—even if one day he does have another family. He won't forget about you."

I rested my head on her shoulder. "How do you know?" I asked her.

"Because I still know your dad better than anyone. I know you mean the world to him. It's breaking his heart to see you like this, Ruby."

I shut my eyes and suddenly I felt terribly, terribly tired. "I'm sorry, Mum," I said. "I'm really sorry."

"Don't you be sorry, darling," Mum said softly. "You have nothing to be sorry about."

Chapter Fourteen

I watched Brett's profile, her face tipped back under the glare of the huge makeup light that was angled directly above her. Her personal makeup artist, Claire, was applying her foundation. It took a long time. Brett had once told me that over their professional relationship, she and Claire had developed a lengthy routine that minimized shadows, reduced lines, and made her look ten years younger than the thirty-nine she actually was. Mind you, Brett told me that about two years ago and she's *still* thirty-nine according to the *Sunday Express* magazine, so I'm not exactly sure how she works it out. Maybe it's like dog years. Maybe there are five human years to every Brett year. It was probably the journalist's fault. They are always printing lies about Brett.

Claire looked annoyed. Claire always looks annoyed, and I'm sure she doesn't appreciate enough what Brett has done for her. I often heard her swearing loudly in complaint about something Brett has done or said, as if it wasn't Brett who paid her wages. And once I caught Claire doing an impression of Brett that made her look like a wicked old witch! That was unfair because, after all, without Brett, Claire wouldn't have a job. In fact, Brett could make it so that Claire never worked in this industry again if she wanted to. Claire is very lucky that Brett is so kind to her.

You see, a lot of people don't see the real Brett. The touchy, hard, nasty Brett isn't her at all. Deep down, she's very kind and vulnerable. I saw her say that on a talk show once. And when she's being Angel's mum, you just know it's true. Sometimes I've even wished Brett *was* my mum.

"Oh, hurry up, Claire!" Brett demanded. "I feel like I've been here for hours!"

Claire rolled her eyes and winked at me. "You *have* been here for hours," she said. "It takes hours to get you looking exactly the way you want to, Brett. It'd be quicker to have a face-lift. Another one."

I was surprised that Claire hadn't read Brett's autobiography, where she says once and for all that she's never had any plastic surgery. I was also surprised that Brett didn't sack her right on the spot. Instead she just looked sideways at me and pursed her lips.

"You don't know how lucky you are," she said, as if she might be quite angry with me. She had every right to be, as ever since I found out I was still on the show, I hadn't had a chance to thank her for her help. That was why I'd hung around after my own makeup had been done, waiting for the right moment to talk to her.

"I know," I said, glancing at my reflection in the mirror. "Mind you, it doesn't take long to get some spots glued on and a bit of grease sprayed in your hair."

I sighed and picked up one of my newly lank strands of hair. Liz said it was so that when I shot my transformation scenes next week, the contrast between the old Angel and the new Angel would be even more dramatic. Which was fair enough, I supposed; it was just that I'd got used to being told I wasn't *beautiful* enough. It was a bit of a shock to be told now I wasn't *ugly* enough. And, what's more, I had to go around like this in front of Justin, who never had to look ugly— who, even with all the special ugly makeup in the world, could never look ugly because his inner beauty just shines through.

Anyway, I made myself concentrate on what I wanted to say to Brett, and not on Justin's inner beauty. I watched as Claire began to stick Brett's false eyelashes on with tweezers and some glue.

"Brett, I've been meaning to say, I know it was all because of you that Liz let me stay on the show and—"

"Ouch!" Brett shot up in her chair as Claire, who had suddenly started choking, accidentally poked her in the eye with the tweezers.

"Sorry, Brett," Claire said between coughs. "Must be my asthma." She took a deep breath and sort of shook herself. "Just lie back and relax." Brett scowled but still didn't fire her.

"Anyway," I continued, "I wanted to say thank you. Thank you *so much* because, well, things have been really difficult recently at home. The last thing I needed was to be thrown off the show too. This is all that's keeping me going."

"I know, darling, I know," Brett said. "Which is exactly why I fixed for—ow!" Brett covered one eye with her hand and the other one glowered at Claire. "I swear, Claire, you are this far from getting the sack."

Claire just shrugged. "I'm always 'this far' from getting the sack," she said. "But you and I both know that I'm the last person in the industry who'll put up with you—and that's only because you pay three times as much as anyone else."

I almost said something to Claire then. I couldn't believe that Brett was letting her get away with being so rude. But the thing about Brett is she's too kind. She lets people take advantage of her. I read that in her autobiography too. She's really too nice for her own good, which is why she's been married so many times. She just can't say no.

"Um, Brett?" I asked her. "What did you mean that you already know?"

"I knew you were worried about leaving the show, darling," Brett said.

"You didn't know that Mum and Dad have split up, then? Because I didn't tell anyone except my friend Nydia."

Brett's face remained expressionless as Claire plucked a stray hair from her eyebrows.

"Your mum and dad have split up?" Claire asked me. She put down her tweezers and gave me a big, impulsive hug. "Oh, Ruby, you poor thing," she said. "My mum and dad split up when I was about your age. I really thought it was the end of the world. It was horrible, but I got through it in the end. I think the important thing to remember is—"

"Oh, shut up, Claire. Ruby is talking to me, not you," Brett said shortly. Claire pressed her lips together as if she were trying to stop something really bad from getting out of her mouth.

"Yes, darling," Brett said to me sweetly. "Of course I did. Well, I mean, I knew that something was wrong, even if I didn't know exactly what. How many times have I said it, Ruby? You're like a daughter to me, after all."

Brett brushed Claire away and beckoned for me to go to her side. She slid her arm around my waist and squeezed me tightly. "But I wish you *had* told me, darling, and Liz too. Because I'm worried about you. With all this going on at home, will you be able to concentrate on your work? Should you even be trying to?"

Brett squeezed me again and I felt some of my bones crack. Then she lowered her voice the way Angel's mum does when she's giving Angel some really good advice. "Maybe a break from work is what you need after all. If you'd like, I could talk to Liz again . . ."

Her smile was kind, but I shook my head quickly. "No! No, I mean, thanks, but no," I said, finding myself wishing she'd stop squeezing me. "I need to work. I need something else to think about. But thank you, Brett. I really mean it."

Brett let go of me at last and I let out a deep breath.

"Brett!" one of the runners called through the door. "On the set in two minutes!"

"OK, OK!" Brett growled back. "These little people," she said. "They have no respect for talent. Claire, sort out my lips. Pronto!"

I looked at my watch as I left makeup and decided to try to fit in a cup of tea before I was needed on the set. But just as I was leaving, Liz grabbed me.

"Ah, Ruby, good. Glad I've found you." She beamed at me. "I was wondering if you'd do a last-minute run-through with Danny. I think he's feeling rather nervous, it being his first day of filming. I thought a familiar face might calm him down a bit and help him get into the swing of things. We've got two scenes with Brett before we need you, so you'll have plenty of time. Do you mind?"

I thought about being shut away with miserable Danny, who hates me so much he can barely talk to me, and I sighed on the inside. I *did* mind, but I'd get over it.

"Not at all," I said, and I trotted off obediently behind her. Liz took me to one of the small rehearsal rooms where Danny was sitting on a table, waiting, and chewing his thumb.

"OK, I'll leave you to it and give you a shout when you're on," she said with a smile, and shut the door behind her.

I went and opened the window looking out onto the lot below, where someone was choreographing the extras for a street scene. You wouldn't think it took so much practicing, would you? Walking around, that is.

"Are you OK?" Danny asked, sounding strangely nice and concerned. "You look terrible!"

My heart sank. "It's makeup," I explained with an embarrassed smile. "At least, mostly."

Danny, on the other hand, *didn't* look terrible. The makeup department had spiked up his black hair and put their special boys' makeup on him, which made him look like he didn't have any makeup on at all—and which really made his blue eyes stand out. I wondered if he had mascara on, but thought it probably wasn't a good idea to ask. He wasn't the sort of boy who shared information like that—or any information at all, in fact.

I decided I'd better start things off. "So, Liz says you're feeling a bit nervous. Don't worry, I was really nervous to begin with," I told him sympathetically before realizing that that wasn't strictly true. "Actually, I wasn't—not to begin with—because I was only little and I didn't really get it. When I was about eleven, then I started to get nervous. But I'm back to being fine with it now." Then I remembered my forthcoming kiss scene. "Well, mostly. I do get a bit nervous still, though. Terrified sometimes!" I laughed, but Danny didn't even smile.

"I'm not nervous," he said shortly. "It's . . . well, it's not how I expected it to be. They film all the scenes out of sync and the scripts come at you like they're rolling off a production line. You never get a chance to really get into a scene—to really get into your character. I mean, what does my character really *think* and *feel*? What's my motivation?"

He looked at me with those intense blue eyes and I felt like a rabbit must when it's caught in the glare of car headlights—like I knew I was going to get run over, but I wasn't exactly sure how to get out of the way.

"Um," I said. "Well, I know what you mean, but that's just how it is in TV . . ." I trailed off. After all, I had grown up on the show; it was the only job I'd done out-side school. I didn't even know there *was* another way to work. It had never occurred to me that the shooting schedule was interfering with my motivation. Angel was like a second skin. I just slipped her on when I needed to, and I knew exactly what she was thinking and feeling, and how she'd react to a scene, because I knew her inside out. We were like two sides of the same coin. Maybe Danny just had to get to know his character better.

"After a while it gets easier," I said. "It's like learning to ride a bicycle, really!"

Danny glared at me and I got the feeling that if I *had* been a rabbit, I'd be a squashed one by now. "Acting is a craft, Ruby," he said. "It's nothing like 'riding a bicycle.' I thought *you* of all people would understand that!"

I was shocked. "You did?" I asked him. I would never have guessed that Danny had ever thought anything about me at all.

"Yes, I did. I thought you weren't like the other girls, more worried about being famous and what they look like than about doing good work and really getting into a character. I must have been wrong."

I scowled at him. "So if all this," I gestured around me, "is *so* terrible, then why are you doing it? Why are you lowering yourself to my level? Why did you audition at all?"

For some reason Danny suddenly blushed, and a deep red tide spread across the bridge of his nose and over his cheeks.

"Um, well, I . . ." He looked at his feet. "Because I know that if I get TV work, it will open up doors for me," he said quickly. "Because I have to—for my career."

"Well," I said haughtily, "I'm sorry you have to put

yourself through the trauma of working with lowlifes like me. But, if you can manage it, we might as well rehearse this scene since we're here. It might help you find your 'motivation.'"

And we read through the scene—which was about Angel making Marcus a cup of tea—as if we were arch-enemies plotting each other's violent demise.

Chapter Fifteen

I was still fuming about Danny as I dried my hair after filming had finished. I was thinking to myself, *Just who does Danny Harvey think he is anyway?* I flicked back my hair, only to see Justin leaning against the door frame, all casual, as if he walked into my dressing room every day. I dropped the hair dryer. Then I picked it up and turned it off.

"Oh, Justin," I said. "Hi."

"Hi, babe," Justin said. (He called me *babe*!) "Great work on the set today. I thought you managed to pull off Angel's instant dislike for Marcus really well. Even just making him a cup of tea, you managed to show that you hated him."

I felt that this would be a good time to flutter my

eyelashes, but the only time I'd ever tried before, Nydia said I looked like I had a nervous twitch.

"Oh, thanks," I said. "It was nothing really." I tried to sound nonchalant, as if the love of my life wasn't talking to me on my own for practically the first time ever. And I was doing pretty well, if nonchalant meant sounding like a million volts of electricity had passed through my body.

"So, listen . . ." Justin came into my tiny dressing room and stood really close to me. For one terrifying and amazing moment I thought he might kiss me then and there and I wouldn't have to worry about going over to Anne-Marie's tonight after all.

But he didn't. "I read our new scenes together. They're great, aren't they? It looks like your character's really going places. I think Liz has got big plans for you."

I couldn't actually say anything, so I tried raising an eyebrow mysteriously. I don't think Justin noticed.

"And I was thinking, well, we don't hang out that much, do we?" Justin continued. "Off the set, I mean."

I shook my head. If I could have spoken, I'd have said that we don't hang out that much *on* the set, except for when we have a scene together, but I couldn't make my mouth work.

Justin smiled. "So I was thinking we should spend some time together. After all, this is a big deal for you. I want you to feel completely comfortable with me."

Of course, I could never feel comfortable with Justin. He makes me feel like fizzing and exploding and looping the loop.

"What about lunch? Just you and me. Tomorrow?" Justin said, as if he asked me out every night of the week. "Will your mum let you go?"

"Oh, yeah, no problem," I finally managed to say. There was no way in the *world* my mum would let me go out on my own with an older boy without an adult accompanying me, but I'd worry about that later.

"Great." Justin's eyes burned into mine, and I thought there was a serious chance I might burst into flames. "We'll sort the details out later, then, OK?"

As he left, it was as if the oxygen flooded back into the room and I was able to breathe again. Justin had asked me out! On a date! More or less. I squealed and hopped around in a tiny circle of joy, which was all I could manage in my dressing room.

"Liz told him to take you out," Danny said, appearing like the angel of gloom at my doorway.

I froze mid-hop and straightened myself out, hoping to salvage some dignity.

149

"It was her idea; she thought you might be nervous about the big kiss scene. She thought that if you spent some time with him you'd be less intimidated." He crossed his arms over his chest and tipped his head to one side. "Looks like she didn't have anything to worry about. The last thing you seem to be is nervous."

"I *am* nervous actually!" I said crossly, just managing not to add "So there!" to the end of my sentence. "Anyway, even if Liz *did* tell him to ask me, I don't care, because . . . well, because I don't care. It's just work."

Danny smirked at me.

"Oh, Danny, go away!" I blurted out. "I've got enough going on right now without you being all sulky around me. Go and be miserable on your own." I clapped my hand over my mouth. "I'm sorry," I said quickly. "That's not like me at all. I don't know what—"

"Don't worry," Danny said. He stepped inside the room and pushed the door closed. "I came to say *I'm* sorry to *you,* anyway. I heard today about your mum and dad. You're right—the last thing you need is hassle from me. I didn't even mean what I said anyway; I was just . . . nervous." He smiled ruefully (and kind of sweetly, to be honest). But I was still trying to work out what he'd just said.

"You heard about Mum and Dad?" I asked him. "But I haven't told anyone except for Brett and . . . oh, it must have been Claire. She must have told everyone." My shoulders sank. "I didn't want anyone to know. Does *everyone* know?"

"Well, I'm not sure," Danny said. "But to be honest, probably everyone does know. I heard it from the dog trainer."

I sighed and started to pack my bag so I'd be ready when Mum came to get me.

"It's so *embarrassing*," I said. "Everyone knowing that my mum and dad can't stand each other—that the happy family they thought I had was all a lie. It was only last year that all three of us were in a *Radio Times* feature about soap kids' everyday lives."

Danny smiled. "Yeah, I saw that. And I know, it's a total nightmare," he agreed. I looked at him questioningly. "My mum and dad split last year," he explained. "Just before the school play, actually. They both came to see it on different nights. Mum brought her new boyfriend." His brows furrowed at the memory.

"Oh!" Suddenly it all made sense: Danny refusing to speak to anyone last year, suddenly getting all mean and moody, how he stopped having a laugh with the other boys and flirting with all the girls. We all put it down to him being stuck-up and full of himself, but really he'd been hurting and lonely—just like me, except he didn't have anyone to talk to.

"I never knew," I said.

"No, well, I didn't want anyone to know, did I? Like you said, it's embarrassing." Danny bit his lip for a moment before adding, "If you ever want to talk to someone about it . . . well, you know."

I wasn't sure I did know, but I nodded anyway.

"Thanks," I said.

"Good. Listen, about having lunch with Justin . . ."

I rolled my eyes. "What about it," I said with a sigh.

"Well, just be careful, OK? You know what he's like."

I stared at Danny. Just when I thought he was actually quite nice, he said something like that about Justin, who was trying to be kind to me.

"Yes, I do know what he's like; I know him much better than you do! You've only been here for five minutes!"

Danny's face fell and he headed for the door. "Whatever," he said over his shoulder.

Then he slammed the door behind him.

The Foundry
Little Frog Lane
Much Hockton
Suffolk

Dear Ruby Parker,

I'm writing to you to ask you how to become famous. I thought if you can become famous, then anybody can—so that's why I chose you to ask. I have always wanted to be famous for as long as I can remember. It's my lifelong dream. (I am now twelve.) I think I would be good at being famous too because I'm outgoing and I like to be the center of attention. I think some people are just special and I'm one of them.

I can't sing very well or act much—or dance, but I don't think it matters. If you really want something, you can make it happen. And there are plenty of pop stars these days who can't sing, aren't there?

Please can you give me some advice? I think you are great on the show—a real inspiration for people like me.

Lots of love,
Bonnie Bond

Ruby Parker

Dear Bonnie,

Thank you for your letter. I think it's great that you are so full of confidence and know exactly what you want in life.

I was very lucky to get the part in Kensington Heights at such a young age, but it takes a lot of hard work and dedication to keep it! I train very hard at school doing all the normal studying you do, and then all my dancing, acting, and singing lessons on top of that. Then I work very hard on the show during my school holidays. I don't have too much time to myself!

My advice to you is to work very hard at school and try to find out what you do have a special talent for. If in a few years you haven't found anything and you still want to be famous, perhaps you could try being a television presenter.

Keep watching the show.

Best wishes,

I reread the letter that Mum had asked me to sign after we'd had dinner. "But I wouldn't have written *that*!" I protested, putting the unsigned letter down on the kitchen table.

"I know you wouldn't, which is why I wrote it for you," Mum said, holding out the pen. "You've got a great big pile of letters in your bedroom waiting to be answered and you're so busy right now that I thought I'd just do a few of the less personal ones for you, that's all. It gave me something else to think about."

It was true; I did have a lot of unanswered letters, including Naomi's, which was still tucked away inside my pillowcase waiting for me to reply. I looked out the kitchen door and up at the sky. I wondered what Naomi was doing tonight. I wondered how she was feeling.

"I wouldn't have even answered Bonnie's letter," I said. "Or if I had, I'd have told her where to—"

"Ruby!" Mum almost laughed. "Just sign the letter, darling, please. Bonnie's only a little girl with hopes and dreams like everyone else. Everyone should be allowed to have a dream—even if some of them don't come true. You don't know how lucky you are sometimes."

I signed the letter and looked up at her.

"I don't feel lucky, Mum," I said. Mum leaned over, put her arm around my shoulders, and gave me a hug.

"I know you don't, darling, but you are," she said

into my hair. "Your mum and dad love you, you haven't got to worry about money, where you're going to sleep, or what you're going eat. You've got a job that millions of little girls like Bonnie would love to do, and you go to a school that most people only dream about. You are very, very lucky, Ruby. Try to remember that, OK?"

I put my arms around her waist and hugged her too. "I would give all of that up, Mum, just to have Dad living with us again." I looked up at her as a terrible thought popped into my head. "Maybe . . . do you think if I hadn't been in the show and if I'd gone to a normal school and we were just ordinary like everyone else, that maybe you and Dad would still be together? Maybe I took too much out of the family."

Mum kissed the top of my head. "That's not true, Ruby," she said gently. "It wouldn't matter what you were doing or where you went to school. None of this is your fault. None of this is about you."

I don't know where it came from, or even what made it happen, but suddenly the sadness I had been feeling turned into cold, hard anger. I pulled away from her hug. "I wish you'd stop saying that!" I yelled. "Of course it's about me. It's my life too! You and Dad are the only ones getting to do what you want. It *is* about me. It *is*!"

Mum sat down at the kitchen table and ran her fingers through her hair. "I'm sorry, Ruby. That's not what I meant. I realize that this affects you too. What I meant was that none of it has happened *because* of you."

"I know that," I said. "But it is happening *to* me just as much as it's happening to you. More so because you don't even seem to care!"

My mum bowed her head. "I *do* care, love . . ." she began, her voice wobbling.

"No, no you don't. All you can say is how it'll all be fine and work out for the best and that one day I'll understand. You don't care at all!"

"I *do* care!" my mum shouted very loudly, making me take a step back. She pushed back the kitchen chair with a scrape and stood up. "I *do* care! I was just trying . . . trying to be strong for you. For *you*, Ruby." Her face had gone all red and she was crying again; tears were streaming down her face. She stretched out her arms to me, but I didn't move, even though I wanted to.

"I have to go out," I said. My voice sounded far away and like cold, hard ice. "I'm going to Anne-Marie's from school. Nydia's dad is bringing us back, OK?"

Mum dropped her arms to her sides and sat back down. "Please, Ruby, don't be angry with me," she sobbed.

"I'm not," I said stiffly. "I'll be home by nine. Bye."

I felt bad as I shut the door behind me. I felt like going back and telling her I was sorry and I didn't mean any of it. But I didn't. I felt so angry, so powerless. I felt like hurting my mum and dad was the only thing I could do to make them see how much they were hurting me.

Chapter Sixteen

I 'm *not* kissing *him*!" I protested, gesturing at Michael Henderson, who was slouched up against the window in Anne-Marie's bedroom. He looked at me and raised an eyebrow. Yuck. "And, anyway, are you mad? You want me to practice kissing on *your* boyfriend?"

Anne-Marie tossed her blonde curls out of her face and gave a short bark of a laugh.

"Oh, don't worry," she scoffed, looking me up and down. "I'm not too worried about the competition."

I squirmed and looked to Nydia for some support. She shrugged and looked apologetic. "Well, Anne-Marie does have a point," she said cautiously. "If you want to be good at kissing, then, you know, you have to practice on someone."

Michael gave me his best smile and my stomach fluttered, but only from queasiness. It wasn't that he was ugly, exactly. It was more that he was too perfect. Like a muscular guy.

I shook my head in disbelief. "I can't believe you're agreeing with her!" I gestured at Anne-Marie, who had crossed her skinny arms over her bony chest and was tapping her foot furiously.

"I'm not agreeing with her *exactly* . . . I'm just saying that she does have a point!" Nydia exclaimed, sounding slightly impatient. "Really, Rube, after all the trouble I've gone through to get you here, you could try not being so . . . well, being a bit . . . It's just that sometimes you can be . . ."

"Be what?" I demanded.

"A bit of a drama queen, OK?" Nydia finally admitted, looking guilty.

"Thank you!" Anne-Marie said, clapping her hands together. "Someone is finally making sense." Nydia couldn't help looking pleased that Anne-Marie had actually said something halfway nice to her.

Anne-Marie marched over to where I was standing. "Listen," she said, putting her face close to mine. "You asked me to help you and I'm helping you. You want to learn how to kiss? Fine. I'll try to achieve the impossible and teach you how to kiss. But how exactly did you think I was going to do that? Did you think I was going to draw you a picture?"

I scowled at her, but I had to admit I hadn't actually thought that far ahead. To be perfectly honest, I didn't think the picture idea was so bad—especially when Michael Henderson was the alternative.

"You might have," I said defensively, looking at her boyfriend with suspicion. He obviously thought he was the best thing ever, but he didn't even compare to Justin. "Anyway—Michael Henderson? I mean, he's your *boyfriend*!"

I knew that when I had a boyfriend—correction, when *Justin* was my boyfriend—I wouldn't be hiring him out to the first girl who needed to learn how to kiss. I'd cherish him and we'd be together—just us, forever.

"I know that, lamebrain!" Anne-Marie snapped back at me. Then she looked over at Michael as if she wished for a second that he wasn't her boyfriend after all. "Luckily for you, he loves me enough to help me out when I ask him—even if it *does* mean he has to get close to you. Anyway, the rules are no touching and no tongue. It's like a technical take for a lighting rehearsal. Just the moves and the positions. None of the heavy stuff."

"Oh, shame!" Michael said with a grin, pretending to be disappointed. Anne-Marie shot him a look so poisonous I was surprised he didn't drop dead that instant. I examined him with a sideways glance. Like I said, I supposed he was quite nice and everything: tall with wavy hair and friendly brown eyes. I could see why Anne-Marie went out with him and why Menakshi would like to steal him away from her if she could, but he wasn't *my* type. He was so into himself. He didn't seem to have any real personality at all—like he just sprayed it on every morning from a can labeled "future celebrity." Most importantly, he wasn't Justin. And, after all, the whole point was that I wanted *Justin* to be my first kiss—not somebody else's bullied boyfriend. I don't think Nydia and I had thought this plan through nearly enough.

"It's all right, Rube," Michael said, winking at me. "I don't mind giving you a snog if it'll help get you going. I've always thought others should benefit from my expertise, and I enjoy a challenge."

Anne-Marie glowered at him and he blanched almost completely white. "No one is going to be enjoying anything, understand?" she growled. "Now listen, Ruby, everyone's first kiss is rubbish anyway. It's a known fact."

"Is it?" asked Nydia glumly. "How disappointing.

You wait years and years for something and then it's rubbish. Typical."

"Yeah, is it?" Michael said to Anne-Marie, looking slightly offended. "You never complained at the time."

Anne-Marie shuddered like a wet dog shaking itself dry.

"Ugh, it was dreadful. All dribbly and toothy— totally disgusting!" she told us frankly.

"Oh, thanks a bunch!" Michael said. He'd stopped looking white with fear and was starting to go bright red with embarrassment. Not such a smooth operator after all.

"Relax, idiot," Anne-Marie told him, rolling her eyes. "It wasn't with *you*!"

Nydia giggled and clapped her hand over her mouth. She was loving Anne-Marie talking to her so much that she'd forgotten the real reason we were here.

"Oh," Michael said, looking relieved, and then, "Oh!"

Anne-Marie ignored him. "Anyway, my point is that it's better to get it out of the way now so when you and Justin have your kiss, it will be perfect." She smiled at me. "Well, as perfect as it can be when a super hunk has to snog a manky old trout like you," she finished cheerily.

"Well, I'd rather be a manky old trout than . . .

than . . ." I spluttered. It was no good. That witty one-liner simply wouldn't come out. Anne-Marie laughed in my face.

"Than what? Than beautiful? Than popular? Than have more than one useless friend? If you'd rather be *you,* then why are you here at all? Why do you need *me*?"

I opened my mouth and shut it again. I was so angry that I thought I was going to ignite with fury. But instead, when I heard myself speak, my voice was low and as cold as ice. I took a step nearer to Anne-Marie.

"I don't need you, Anne-Marie. And Nydia doesn't need you either." I looked her up and down. "We're here because we thought you could help me with something I thought was important. But do you know what you've made me realize? Nothing is so important that I have to listen to you slag off my best friend. Nydia is worth a thousand of you. She is a kind and generous person—a person who'd be your friend even after all the things you've said and done to her. She's a person who'd always be there for you if you needed her, and always listen to you even if most of the time you talked rubbish. But you just throw all that back in her face, time after time. I don't care if you tell the whole school about this; I don't care if everyone laughs at me for the rest of my life. I'd rather have Nydia as my friend than be in the same room with you for one second longer. You're just a nasty, spoiled, arrogant, heartless cow—so mean and spiteful that even your own family doesn't want to live with you. You don't know what real friendship is." I picked up my bag. "Come *on*, Nydia, we're going."

But Nydia didn't move. Instead she looked anxiously at Anne-Marie, whose evil-genius face had crumpled a bit. "Come *on*, Nydia!" I said. She was taking the wind out of my dramatic exit.

Nydia went over to Anne-Marie. "Are you OK?" she asked her.

My jaw dropped. "What do you mean is *she* OK? Come on, let's go!"

Nydia shook her head and I looked at Anne-Marie. I could see she was shaking, that her lips were pressed tightly together and her eyes were glittering with tears. She was trying not to cry. But she was. I'd made Anne-Marie Chance cry but, strangely, instead of feeling triumphant about it, I felt rather uncomfortable and guilty.

Nydia put her hand on Anne-Marie's shoulder. "Ruby didn't mean any of that stuff she said, you know," she told Anne-Marie gently.

"Uh, I did, actually," I pointed out, but Nydia ignored me.

"She did," Anne-Marie agreed, sniffling. "And she's right. My parents don't want to live with me."

"I'm sure they do!" Nydia said hastily. "Is that why you're upset? Because of what Ruby said about your parents? Not all the other stuff?"

Anne-Marie lifted her chin defiantly. "That's all true too," she said, "but I don't care."

"Don't you?" Nydia asked. "It's just that it's hard to understand sometimes why you hate us so much." Her brows furrowed and she continued softly. "What gives you the right to talk to us the way you do, call us names, make things up about us and get all your friends to ignore us? What have we ever done to you?"

Anne-Marie rubbed her eyes with the heels of her palms. "Go on, tell us," Nydia said, "because I'd really like to know."

Michael took a cautious step closer to Anne-Marie and Nydia. I think he could sense some serious girls' stuff approaching.

"So . . . should I go, then?" he asked awkwardly. "I mean, if you're going to do all this girly stuff? I'll just leave, shall I?"

Anne-Marie turned her face away from him. "Yes, just go, Michael," she said. "Just go." He sloped out of her room, winking at me as he left. He wouldn't win any awards for being a supportive boyfriend, that's for sure.

Anne-Marie looked at me and then Nydia. "It's you two," she said. "You think you're so special—better than the rest of us."

I nearly fell over with surprise.

"Pardon?" I asked sarcastically. "I think you'll find that's you." Nydia shot me a look and I shrugged. "Well, it's true," I mumbled.

"No," Anne-Marie said, looking right at me. "It's *you*—especially you—the TV star. You swan around school like you own the place, like you're better than everybody else because you've already made it. And you're always going on and on about how many fan letters you have to answer each week or what you have to wear to an awards ceremony, and complaining because people stop you in the street and ask for your autograph! Poor little you. Boo hoo." She sniffed and sat up a little straighter.

"I don't!" I protested, looking at Nydia and wondering exactly why we hadn't made our exit when we should have, right after my brilliant speech. "I mean, I sometimes talk about it to Nydia because, well, it really *can* be hard sometimes. I don't do it to show off. I don't do it like that!" I looked at Nydia. "Do I?"

She pursed her lips and looked at the ceiling for a second. "Sometimes, you might come across a bit like that—even if you don't mean to." She added on the

167

last bit hurriedly. "I think it's sort of a defense mechanism."

"Nydia, I don't!" I glanced at Anne-Marie, who was looking decidedly self-righteous.

"Look," Nydia said. "All I'm saying, Ruby, is that in a room full of people who'd give their right arm to be doing what you're doing, moaning because people ask you for your autograph could *possibly* be considered to be a bit . . . stuck-up." Then she gave me a huge grin as if she had just said something completely different.

"You're supposed to be on *my* side," I said, feeling hurt and confused. "I just stood up for you. Big time!"

"I know," Nydia said, crossing the room to where I stood. "And that was really cool. It meant a lot to me, Ruby. It's just—wouldn't it be better at school if we could get along with everyone else? I'm tired of being treated like I'm nothing. I just thought that maybe . . ." Nydia shrugged and trailed off.

"OK," I said. "OK, maybe I do come across like that. But what about you, Anne-Marie? What about all the horrible things you've said to me and to Nydia? We don't deserve any of that." I gestured around at her huge bedroom. "I mean, look at all this! You've got everything anyone could want. You don't even have to try to get what you want; your daddy will just give it to you. You've got *everything*."

Anne-Marie shook her head and dropped her chin, mumbling something under her breath.

"Pardon?" I asked impatiently.

"No, I haven't," Anne-Marie said a little louder. "I haven't got everything anyone could want. I've a big house and lots of things, that's true. But I've got all this *instead* of the things you have. You were right about my parents. Do you know the last time I saw my mum? February—for forty-two minutes in the Heathrow first-class lounge, in between one flight coming and one going. She gave me a bottle of Ralph Lauren perfume for my birthday. My birthday isn't until August, but I won't be seeing her before then, apparently."

Nydia and I looked at each other. That was pretty harsh.

"And my dad is always in LA. I mean, he's supposed to come back and see me once a month—and he does come back to England—but he's always out wheeling and dealing and seeing all his contacts and working. I see him for about half an hour a day while he's here, if I'm lucky, and even then he's usually on the phone. My parents don't even see each other. And my brother— well, he's old enough to be able to get out, and he does. That just leaves me and Pilar alone in this house. And Pilar's great, but it's not the same as having a mum to talk to."

I thought about the way I used to tell my mum everything and I almost felt sorry for Anne-Marie. It was strange seeing her like this—one minute being her good old evil self, the next looking and acting like, well, a normal girl.

"But I thought you said you liked it," I asked the normal-girl version, cautiously. "You said you could do what you want."

Anne-Marie sighed. "It's no fun being able to do what you want when there's no one around to tell you not to," she said.

Nydia sat next to her on the bed. "I'm sorry," Nydia said. "That must be hard. I don't know what I'd do without my mum and dad."

I sighed. I supposed I knew deep down that Mum and Dad *did* love me, even if it looked like they really weren't going to be together anymore. At least I knew if I needed one or both of them, they'd be there for me. If what she said was true, Anne-Marie didn't have that.

"I'm sorry too," I said hesitantly. "Parents are a nightmare, aren't they? Nydia thinks hers are too lovey-dovey and mine are splitting up."

Anne-Marie looked at me. "Oh, I didn't know, Ruby. That must be tough," she said with concern. I covered my surprise.

"It's all right," I said. "But, anyway, having stupid

parents doesn't make it OK for you to pick on us, does it? It's not a good reason. I've got stupid parents and you don't see me going around making you cry . . ." I looked at Anne-Marie's tearstained face. "Much. I mean, which Anne-Marie is the real Anne-Marie? The one who goes parading around school like the Queen of Sheba? Or you, like you are now? Nice. Ish."

"I don't know," Anne-Marie finally said after a long pause. She looked up at Nydia. "Everyone—all the girls, I mean—expects me to be a certain way. Everyone expects me to be funny and the leader. You two—you're just easy targets, that's all. And, well, you make it easy. Especially you, Nydia. You never fight back. You're too nice."

Nydia's eyes widened. "You hate me because I'm too *nice*?" she asked in disbelief. "Not because I'm fat, or black, or don't live in a big house like yours. You hate me because I'm nice?" Nydia shook her head. "I don't understand. Why would anybody hate someone because they're nice? Are you saying that if I was cruel and a bully like you and your friends that you'd like me? Is that what you're saying?"

Anne-Marie shifted uncomfortably on the bed. "I . . . no . . . I don't know, OK? Sometimes you can sort of forget a person has feelings. You sort of forget they're real, and being mean becomes a habit." Anne-Marie

171

bit her lip and held out a hand for Nydia to shake. "I'm sorry, Nydia. I really am. I hear myself sometimes and I think, what a nasty cow! And then I realize that it's *me* talking. I don't know how I got to be like that, but I'm sorry. I really am." Then Anne-Marie looked up at me. "And I'm sorry for what I've done to you too, Ruby. I suppose that . . ." She looked down. "I suppose I was jealous of everything you've got. I suppose that's the real reason I haven't been nice to you. You've got this incredible role and all that fame—everything that I want. But you say you don't know which is the real me? Well, I didn't know the real you, until tonight. I still don't, really."

I plumped down onto the bed and the three of us sat side by side, looking at our feet.

"I'm sorry too," I said after a while, "for calling you all those names. I suppose I don't really know you properly either."

Anne-Marie nodded. "It's like we haven't been going to school together at all!"

We all looked at our feet for a moment longer.

"So what now?" Nydia asked.

"Well, I don't know about you two," I said, "but I think we should call off the kissing practice."

Nydia and Anne-Marie chuckled.

172

"Michael's run a mile anyway," Nydia said. "You must have scared him off, Ruby!"

"It doesn't take much to scare him," Anne-Marie said ruefully. "He's not exactly romantic-hero material. I'm thinking of chucking him anyway. He's nice-looking and everything, but he checks out his reflection more than me."

We all chuckled again.

"Um, I think we should tell you," Nydia said, "as we're making a clean start. We made up the bit about getting you an interview for the show. That was a total lie."

I rolled my eyes. I'm sure we could have left that detail out and it wouldn't have mattered.

"Yeah?" Anne-Marie didn't seem too surprised. "Oh well. I didn't really think you had any influence in casting, Ruby. And I was going to tell everyone about your kissing practice at school anyway."

I thought about being offended, then decided I couldn't be bothered.

"We're idiots, aren't we?" I said. "A bunch of stupid girls behaving like morons."

"Yeah," Nydia said.

"We are," Anne-Marie agreed. Then she paused as if considering something. "I know," she said finally. "Let's send out for pizza and watch DVDs instead."

"Good plan," Nydia and I said together.

Anne-Marie smiled. "Hanging out with two losers—I'm never going to live this down!"

Chapter Seventeen

And from then on, everything started changing. Remember that down escalator that I kept trying to run up, which never got me anywhere? Well, after that night at Anne-Marie's house it changed direction. It started going up and up faster and faster—and even if I wanted to, I couldn't get off.

There was nothing I could do to change my life back to the way it had always been, and there was nothing I could do to stop it from changing—or to stop *me* from changing either. There was no way that Mum and Dad were going to fall back in love with each other, even if they both still loved me; I was slowly beginning to see that. And funnily enough, it was because of Anne-Marie. When she talked about her parents, I could see that my dad *did* love me, even if he couldn't stay when I asked him. I was still angry with him—still angry that he couldn't just stay at home and keep things the way they used to be—but I knew he loved me and that I was lucky. Because when the anger and the hurt had died down, he would still love me. I was luckier than Anne-Marie and I was luckier than Naomi, whose letter I still hadn't answered. Neither one of them knew that they were loved like I did.

And I was going to kiss Justin, under studio lights, in front of cast and crew, next to a hydrangea, without any practice and without the faintest idea of what I was doing—and there was nothing, *nothing* I could do about it. I didn't know what waited for me at the top of those escalators, but I thought it was probably a very, very long drop.

When I got back from Anne-Marie's house that night it was way past nine; in fact, it was nearly ten. We'd had a long lecture from Nydia's dad on the way back in the car for not calling him to pick us up until late. I knew I was going to get another talk from my mum the moment I got in, especially considering the way we had parted earlier in the evening. And I was right, except it wasn't about being late.

Mum was standing at the bottom of the stairs when I opened the front door. I wasn't sure if she'd just been passing by or if she'd actually been standing there waiting for me to open it. She crossed her arms and pressed her lips together.

"Sorry I'm late," I said quickly. "We got talking and . . ."

"I've just spoken to Nydia's dad, Rube, so I don't need to hear it."

I shrugged and took off my coat. "OK, I'm sorry. But this girl Anne-Marie, she's got about three hundred DVDs and we were watching this really good film and I forgot what time it was . . ." That was more or less true. I decided to skip the part about me, Nydia, and Anne-Marie screaming and shouting at one another before we finally seemed to become friends. That part I was still trying to understand. I still didn't quite believe it myself.

Mum gave one of her cross shrugs and walked into the living room. I stood stock-still in the hallway. Normally her lectures went on for much longer than this and involved me being grounded. I was confused. Eventually I decided to head to my room and hope she'd forget all about it.

"I spoke to Liz this evening," she called out as I started up the stairs. I stopped. I walked back down and into the living room.

"Oh?" I said. I yawned conspicuously. "Gosh, I'm tired. Silly me for staying out so late. Good night, Mu—"

"Ruby, sit down." Mum's voice was stern but not really angry. I sat down, hoping I'd be allowed out again before I turned sixteen. Sometimes Mum has a way of making me feel in the wrong even when I haven't done anything. "She said she'd been meaning to call me for a couple of weeks now, but after she heard about me and your dad she just had to ring. I'm glad you told her. She's been very supportive of you since you joined the show."

I shrugged and dropped my chin onto my chest. "I know," I said into the neck of my T-shirt. "But I didn't exactly tell her. She just heard. I thought maybe things might change and, well, things at work were a bit up and down and I just didn't say anything . . ." I trailed off.

"Liz was worried about you. She said she'd meant to discuss your new story line with me. Imagine how I felt, Ruby. I had no idea you had a big new story line coming up! She thought you would have told me straightaway; she assumed that if I'd had any questions or worries, I'd have been in touch. She thought we'd have gone through the script together like we always do." Mum looked worried. She brushed a strand of hair away from my face and tucked it behind my ear. "She told me about their plans for you, Ruby. They sound exciting! Why didn't you tell me? Is it because of everything that's being going on here? I understand if it is, but I couldn't bear the thought of you not talking to me anymore. I always thought we could talk about anything. I thought that you told me everything."

I looked up at her. She wasn't angry, I realized. She was hurt and worried once again that somehow she was letting me down.

"I got all worked up about it," I said, "even before I knew about you and Dad. Everything seemed to come at once. I thought they were going to drop me from the show and it seemed like the end of the world, and then Dad moved out and it *was* the end of the world, and then Liz and Trudy came up with this new story line and . . . did Liz tell you about the kissing scene?"

I looked at Mum warily. She was so keen that I shouldn't grow up one second faster than she wanted me to that I thought she'd hate the idea. But, instead, she just laughed.

"Well, yes, but it's not really a kissing scene, is it?" she said, ruffling my hair. "It's more of a scene with a kiss in it."

For some reason her reaction disappointed me.

"Well, I suppose," I said, glumly. "If you put it like that."

She looked closely at me. "Has that been worrying you?" she asked me. "Because if *you* feel you're too young . . ."

"Mum! No," I said, picking up a cushion and hugging it over my tummy. "It's not that I'm too young. I just didn't talk to you about it because I thought you had too much other stuff to worry about."

Mum put her arm around me.

"Ruby, whatever is happening in my life, there will never be a day that I won't be here when you want to talk to me about anything. When you're ninety-five and I'm a decrepit old lady you can *still* tell me everything. OK?"

I had to admit I felt better now that she knew about everything. Well, nearly everything. Talking to a parent or teacher *did* help, after all. Of course, I'd always known that; I'd just forgotten it recently.

Mum kissed the top of my head. "Liz told me Justin was taking you to lunch tomorrow. Is that right?"

I sighed inwardly. She really *did* know everything.

"Yes, but it's only for work—just so we can talk over the scene and everything. It's not as if it's a date!" I rolled my eyes. Mum suppressed a smile.

"Do you have a crush on Justin?" she asked me gently.

I sat up with a start. "No! Anyway, he's got a girl-friend. And I don't fancy him, so I don't even care. It's only work."

Mum nodded.

"OK. Well, if Liz has arranged it, I'm sure it will be fine. You can go."

I headed quickly for the stairs, thanking my lucky stars.

"And on Sunday, you can start being grounded for coming home so late tonight, OK?"

"OK," I answered wearily. I should have known Mum would never let me get away with that.

Chapter Eighteen

I never thought in a million years that Anne-Marie Chance would ever be sitting on my bed putting her glitter gel on my eyelids. It was so strange that if I hadn't been about to go to lunch with the love of my life, and if my stomach hadn't been invaded by a flock of butterflies, I probably would have been quite freaked out by it. Strangely, Everest—who never got excited about anything that wasn't edible— seemed to love Anne-Marie and continuously rubbed his head against her leg. If Everest liked her, she couldn't be all that bad.

"Now, all you need is a touch here and there." She dabbed my closed eyelids. "Just on the inner corner of your eyes. This makes them look bigger and wider apart and also eliminates all those dark shadows." She smiled at me when I opened my eyes. "Not bad," she said, regarding her handiwork.

"How do you know all this stuff?" I asked her. "I know nothing about makeup. I mean, I've read articles and seen what other girls do, but when *I* try to put any on, I end up looking like a clown."

Anne-Marie smiled and shrugged. "I don't know, really; I just seem to pick it up. I have a lot of time to myself, after all." She unzipped her makeup bag. "Now for some lip gloss . . ."

Nydia leaned over Anne-Marie's shoulder and examined me. "You look really nice, Ruby," she said, sounding slightly surprised. Anne-Marie and I laughed.

"Oh, thanks!" I said.

"No, I mean, when Anne-Marie suggested she come over and do your face, I wasn't exactly sure what she meant. Only a week ago it would have meant giving you two black eyes. But you do look really nice." Nydia knelt down on the floor next to my bed. "Will you do my eyes next?" she asked Anne-Marie. "I haven't got a date with the hunkiest bloke in Britain, but I'd like to know about eyeliner all the same."

Anne-Marie laughed. "Sure," she said. Nydia and I exchanged glances. It was so strange. Here she was, being nice to us, doing our makeup and having a laugh, and as far as I could tell she wasn't doing it because of some evil-genius master plan to stop us from thwarting her bid for world domination. This Anne-Marie was a completely different person from the one I'd always known. As usual it was Nydia who put into words what I was thinking.

"Anne-Marie," Nydia said uncertainly, "when we go back to school . . . well, will you still talk to us or will it be back to normal?"

Anne-Marie paused mid–lip gloss and looked at her. "Have you ever seen those wildlife documentaries about dangerous animals, like tigers and stuff?"

Nydia and I exchanged glances.

"Um, yeah," I said, trying to keep my lips from sticking together.

"Well, you know when they tell you if you're ever confronted with an angry tiger you mustn't ever show it you're afraid? That the moment it knows you're scared it'll just rip you to shreds?" She finished glossing my lips.

"Um, yes?" Nydia answered.

"Well, being friends with Jade and Menakshi is a bit like being confronted with an angry tiger. You never know when they're going to sense your insecurities and turn on you. Anyway, I could never talk to them the way I talk to you two." She smiled at us. "So, yes, I know it will be weird and everyone will think I'm a nutter, but I *will* still be talking to you when we go back to school—if you're still talking to me, that is. What Jade and Menakshi will do—who knows. I don't care anymore."

She grinned at us and I realized that not only was Anne-Marie actually nice, she was also really brave. It was much easier to stay on the right side of the tigers than it was just to be yourself.

"Just be yourself," Nydia told me as I stood by the front door. My mum hovered in the kitchen trying really hard not to interfere. "If you're yourself, he can't help but love you."

I widened my eyes and nodded back toward the direction of the kitchen, shaking my head. "Don't be silly, Nydia. I'm only meeting him for work. It isn't a date or anything!" I said loudly for Mum's benefit. "And, anyway," I added, lowering my voice, "I've been myself for the last seven years and he barely even knows who I am."

"He'll notice you today," Anne-Marie said, clapping a hand on my shoulder. "You look great!"

Finally Mum came out of the kitchen.

"You look nice, Ruby," she said. I waited for her to

complain about the glitter gel, but she didn't. She just stood there looking at me like I was some stranger who had replaced her daughter. "Are you sure you don't want me to give you a lift there?" she asked.

I really didn't.

"It's OK, Mum, we're only going to the Italian place down the road. I can walk it in five minutes."

She furrowed her brow, and I knew she was thinking of things to be worried about.

"Don't worry, Mum," I told her. "It's only Justin from work. It's no big deal."

Mum nodded. "OK, well. You're going to see your dad afterward, aren't you?"

I hesitated. Dad had phoned me last night and asked me round to his new place. It felt strange and wrong, but I had agreed to go anyway because at least he was trying.

"Yeah," I said, dropping my chin a little.

"Ruby, be nice to him, OK?" I nodded. "And call me when you've finished lunch, and call me when you get to your dad's, and call me when you're on your way home." I rolled my eyes and opened the door. "Mum, you really worry too much."

"Only because I love you," Mum said, and she watched Nydia, Anne-Marie, and me walk down the garden path.

"Well, good luck, old chap," Nydia said in her mock posh voice. She held out her hand and shook mine firmly, as if I were off to battle.

"Yes, jolly good luck," Anne-Marie said, joining in the game. She gave me a little salute.

"Thanks awfully," I said. "Well, time to go." I smiled at them, gave another little wave over my shoulder. Then we were walking in opposite directions. They headed to Nydia's for lunch and I went to meet my destiny.

"Hi, Ruby!" Cassie smiled at me as I walked into the restaurant. "You look nice today. Are your mum and dad on the way in?"

I shook my head nervously. "No, I'm meeting Justin de Souza here." Cassie looked blank. "From the show? He plays Caspian." Cassie seemed a bit nonplussed, and I realized that she probably hardly ever saw the show, since she was almost always working whenever it was on.

"Ohhh, is he famous, then?" she asked.

"A bit," I said with a smile. "So if you could put us somewhere out of the way, that would be great. He really values his privacy."

"So is this a date?" Cassie teased me.

"Oh, no," I said quickly. "We just have some scenes

coming up that we want to talk over." Cassie looked like she didn't believe a word of it. She seated me in a booth against the far wall of the restaurant. I looked around; it was early—and there weren't many people in yet. Justin had said I should meet him at twelve, but I didn't mind that he was late. It gave me a chance to practice how my face would look when I saw him. I practiced a calm, sophisticated hello as I waited.

After twenty minutes or so, I was really good at it. I looked at my watch.

"Do you want a Coke?" Cassie asked me as she passed.

I shook my head. "No, I'll wait," I said. I'd had visions of us sharing a chilled bottle of champagne, even though I knew that Cassie would never serve us alcohol in a million years. (And, anyway, I'd tried champagne once at an after-show party and it made me gag). But, even so, I didn't want to start without him.

And so I waited for another thirty minutes. Then I pulled out my mobile phone and looked at it. I hadn't had any missed calls. I didn't have Justin's number and I realized he probably didn't have mine either. He'd never asked me for it on Friday when we'd settled on the time—twelve—and this restaurant. *Maybe he said one*, I thought. *Maybe he'll come at one.* So I waited.

But by twenty past one, he still hadn't arrived.

Even though I've been quite a lucky person, I'm not an optimistic one. I always think things are going to go wrong, so that when they don't it's a nice surprise. But all I'd been worried about today was having the right look on my face when Justin arrived. It never occurred to me that he wasn't going to arrive at all. It never occurred to me that, on my very first date, I'd get stood up—even if it wasn't, strictly speaking, a date.

It was a quarter till two when I fully realized what had happened. He wasn't coming. He wasn't delayed, he hadn't said another time, he didn't mean another day or even another place. He just wasn't coming.

I didn't know what to do. I hadn't prepared a face for being stood up. I stared at the tabletop, feeling frozen to the spot. The restaurant was busier now, and if I walked past all these people on my own, then they'd know I'd been stood up.

But then Cassie appeared with a huge smile on her face and I knew that he'd arrived. Justin had actually arrived!

"I hope he's worth the wait!" she said, and she stepped aside to reveal . . .

Danny.

"Danny!" I exclaimed. Just for a second I was

189

disappointed, and then I realized I'd never been so glad to see anyone in my life. I could have flung my arms around his neck and kissed him—if only I'd known how to kiss a boy, that is. He sat down opposite me, his cheeks glowing.

"What are you doing here?" I looked around. The booth was completely secluded. There was no way he could have seen me from the street. He shifted a little in his seat. "You look really . . . nice," he said. "Um, anyway, Justin just called me. He said he'd . . ." Danny looked at me. "He said something really important had come up and he didn't have your number, so he asked me to come by and apologize for him. He knew I lived nearby." Danny dropped his gaze to the cutlery on the table. "He said he's really sorry, so . . ."

I beamed at him. Not only had he saved me from walking out of here on my own, but he'd brought me the news I'd wanted to hear: that Justin hadn't forgotten about me, but that he just couldn't come because of something really, *really* important. And he'd worried about me so much that he'd gone to the trouble of calling Danny and asking him to come and tell me in person. He really cared. I felt all glowy inside. Maybe he was chucking his stupid girlfriend right now.

I looked at my watch. "Oh, well, thanks for letting

me know, Danny," I said. "I'm not supposed to be at my dad's until three. I suppose I could go back home . . ." I thought about my mum and all her questions. Even if *I* knew that Justin technically hadn't stood me up, other people might not see it in quite the same way. I'd have to tell Nydia and Anne-Marie later, I supposed. They would be dying to know how it went. They'd be so disappointed that it was only Danny who'd turned up. Strangely, I wasn't that disappointed.

"Have you eaten?" Danny asked me tentatively. My stomach growled.

"Oh, God, no—I'm starving!" I laughed, and he smiled back at me.

"We could share a pizza if you like." He dug into his pocket and clattered a five-pound note and some change onto the table. "I think I've got enough for half a pizza."

I grinned at him.

"OK," I said. "Why not?"

If I've learned one thing over the last few days it's that people aren't always how they seem. After talking to Anne-Marie, I realized she thought I was a vain cow who loved herself for being on the telly. *Me!* And all this time I'd thought she was a vain cow who loved herself for being thin and pretty. *Her!* And she didn't know that Nydia was a lovely, funny girl with a huge heart and the best imagination for ridiculous plans whom anyone could ever hope to meet. And until I really talked to Anne-Marie—and then Danny—I thought that everyone's parents were like Nydia's: two good friends who loved each other and would always be together. I didn't realize that Nydia's parents are actually really, *really* unusual.

Danny told me all about his parents' divorce and his two bedrooms in two houses, and the every-other-weekend he spends with his dad and his dad's new family.

"Isn't it weird though?" I asked him. "Isn't it horrible?" Danny shrugged and looked up at me through his thick, brown lashes. I'd never noticed them before. My tummy fluttered. It must have been the pizza giving me indigestion. I'd been so hungry that I'd eaten too quickly.

"Oh, well, yes, of course it was weird at first," Danny told me. He had a nice voice, I noticed—sort of gentle and quiet. "But my little stepbrother is quite cool. We have a laugh. And Dad is different now. He used to be angry all the time. Now he's just . . . well, he's just Dad."

I thought about the strain and tension that had

stretched over our house for a long time now. Even with all the pain and change that had come with Dad leaving, at least the tension between him and Mum was gone. I thought I understood what Danny meant.

Danny gave me one of his sweet half-smiles. "It *will* be all right," he said.

"Yes." I sighed. "That's what everyone keeps saying."

"That's because everyone is right," he said. And when *he* said it, I believed it might be true.

We piled all our cash onto the table and even left Cassie a thirty-four–pence tip. And without me asking him to, Danny walked me to my dad's flat. I looked up at the second-floor window where Dad was waiting for me.

"It's funny," I said to Danny. "I've walked past this place hundreds of times and I've never even looked at it. And now this is where my dad lives. This is where I'll be coming to see him. I'm going to get to know this place really well."

I looked up at Danny, who was standing quite close to me. "But I guess it will be all right," I said, remembering what he told me.

"It will," he said. And just then, when he looked at me, I thought he was going to kiss me. I panicked, took a quick step back, and looked around as I felt my cheeks begin to burn.

"Um . . . so . . . anyway, thanks for coming!" I said. "To tell me about Justin, I mean," I added quickly. "Um, so, I'd better go in now."

Danny's face blazed with color. I couldn't decide if I'd imagined that moment or not. I didn't really have any experience with that kind of moment—at least not in real life.

"No problem," he said miserably, looking at the pavement. "Ruby . . . ?"

I backed away from him another couple of steps and looked at the door. My heart was racing.

"Yes?" I asked with a brittle smile. Danny looked up at me and then shook his head.

"Oh, nothing. It doesn't matter. I'll see you on the set." He turned and, shoving his hands deep into his pockets, quickly walked away.

I stood outside the front door and waited for a long time until my heart slowed down and I could breathe again. I didn't understand the heart-thundering, fizzy dizziness. It couldn't have been Danny who made me feel like that. It must have been nerves about seeing Dad in his new place. And indigestion. Nerves and indigestion, that was it.

I looked down the street and saw Danny disappear

around the corner. It couldn't be because of Danny since it was Justin who I was in love with, after all.

At last I rang the doorbell to Dad's flat, and, after a few seconds, I went in. I walked into the place where he now lived without me.

It was all right at Dad's place in the end. For the first few minutes none of it seemed real. And, anyway, half of me was still standing on the pavement outside, wondering if Danny really *had* been about to kiss me—and wondering what would have happened if I hadn't taken that quick step back.

Dad sat me down on a worn-out beige sofa and went into the small kitchen that led off the living room.

"Fancy a juice?" he called out to me.

"Yeah, OK," I said. I looked around. It was a small room with a big bay window wreathed in gray, decaying net curtains that made the room seem darker than it was. It was strange to see Dad's jacket laid across the back of an unfamiliar chair and his shoes kicked under someone else's fold-down table.

"So what do you think?" Dad asked, gesturing around the room.

I looked up at him.

"I don't know," I said honestly. "I suppose it will be

OK once you've cleaned it and taken down those curtains."

Dad sat down next to me and looked at me closely.

"It's OK, Dad," I told him. "I'm not going to cry or anything."

He sort of smiled and handed me a glass of weak orange squash. I looked at it; I hadn't drunk orange squash since I was about eight years old. But I suppose it was never Dad who got me drinks; it was always Mum. Why would he even know? At least now he'd start to learn more things about me—small things he never knew before, like the fact that I only drink *fresh* juice.

"I've missed you," Dad said.

"Have you?" I replied quickly. "I thought you would have been too busy with your girlfriend." I didn't mean to be cruel; it just came out before I could stop it.

Dad sighed. "She's not my girlfriend, Ruby. Sally's just . . . a friend."

I shrugged and chewed my lip. It was weird to be in a strange room, not knowing what to say to my own dad.

"How's Everest?" Dad asked me. "Still eating us out of house and home?" I smiled because only that morning Everest had jumped on the kitchen counter and taken two slices of toast straight out of the toaster. He must be the only cat in the world who loves to hunt bread. That's probably because he's lazy and can't be bothered to chase anything that might actually move.

"Yeah, he is," I said without elaborating. After all, it wasn't "us" Everest was eating out of house and home. It was just me and Mum now.

There was another long moment of silence.

"I heard this great joke this morning. Shall I tell it to you?" Dad asked me hopefully. I looked at him.

"No," I said. His face fell. "No, Dad, it's not that I don't want to hear it, but it's just that . . . well, don't you think it's pointless pretending that all this is fine and normal? It's going to take a long time for me to get my head around this. I *think* I'm beginning to realize that it will be OK in the end, that one day all this will make sense to me and be normal. But it won't happen just like that. I won't just feel better over a glass of orange squash and some bad jokes. There are all these things going through my head, around and around in circles. If we pretend everything's all right, it never will be. We need to talk about it, Dad."

Dad leaned his forehead against mine and put his arm around my shoulder. "You're right, Ruby," he said. "I'm not sure when it was you got so wise, but you're right."

He hugged me close to him and, for the first time since the night he told me he was going, he felt like my dad again.

"And, Dad?" I told him. "I've missed you too."

Dear Naomi,

I'm so sorry it's taken me this long to write back to you. When I first got your letter it felt a bit strange because you were right—I do know what you're going through, but not because of what's happened to Angel on the show. It's because my mum and dad are splitting up too.

It hurts, doesn't it? I know it has hurt me very much. But even though I still wish I could make things go back to the way they were before, I know that I can't. I'm still sad about it—and scared and angry—but at least now I know how things are going to be.

It must be very difficult for you. It sounds like your mum and dad are really angry at each other and they're putting you in the middle of it. I don't think that either one of them really knows how much this is affecting you or your brother. If they did, I'm sure they would stop and try to work things out. It sounds like they don't really think this is happening to you too. You could try to talk to them and explain how you feel, but if they are too angry and too hurt to listen, then find another adult to talk to—someone who will speak to them for you. But most of all, remember that everything that is happening is happening to you, not because of you. It will be all right one day, Naomi. I don't know when, but I know that it will be.

Please write to me again and let me know how you are.

Ruby x

Chapter Nineteen

Claire was finishing off my hair by running a pair of straighteners through it.

"Nervous?" she asked my reflection in the mirror. I thought about it. In about twenty minutes, my lips—Ruby Parker's—would be meeting the lips of Justin de Souza.

"No," I said, and strangely it was true.

Claire smiled and shook her head as if she didn't believe me. "They really think a lot of you here, you know. Don't be nervous: If you can survive Brett, you can survive a kiss scene, believe me."

I frowned at her reflection in the mirror.

"I don't think you should be rude about Brett, Claire," I said. "I know you both have your differences,

200

but . . . well, she's done a lot for me."

Claire set down the straighteners and crossed her arms.

"You really must be an angel, the way you look up to Brett. And after everything she's done to you!" She gave a little shrug. "And, anyway, she doesn't pay my wages anymore. You may have noticed that I'm not exclusively her makeup designer now, which is why I'm doing you today. I resigned and told Liz I'd work on the show only on the condition that I don't have to work with that miserable old cow."

"Claire!" I said, laughing despite myself. I sat up in my chair and looked at myself in the mirror. It didn't really look like me or Angel. They'd put gold highlights through my hair and just enough makeup to make me look, well, kind of pretty. With some carefully applied color on my cheeks, a light lip gloss, and black/brown mascara, I looked nice. It was the sort of thing I'd never be able to do to myself in a million years.

But then I remembered I was sticking up for Brett. "Brett's always been really good to me."

Claire brandished some hairspray at me.

"You still believe that?" she said. "Even after Brett demanded that you be fired from the show or she was leaving?"

"Look, no matter what you think of her—" Claire's

words caught up with my ears and my jaw dropped. "Wait . . . what?" I exclaimed. I couldn't believe what I had just heard.

Claire looked at me with disbelief. "You honestly didn't know, did you? You poor kid." She leaned back against the dressing table. "God only knows how you don't—it was all over the set! Everyone can see that Brett hasn't got it anymore. She drinks all the time and swans around like she owns the place. The public doesn't care about her. Everyone knows she's jealous of all the young talent. She heard that Liz and Trudy wanted to build your part and she couldn't stand it. She told them it was *her* or *you*. I heard they did discuss giving in to her because, after all, it was Brett who was the star in the beginning. But then she pushed her luck too far with Liz, and Liz put her in her place. She looks likes a pussycat, Liz does, but she's got a tiger lurking in there too. So, anyway—they chose you."

My mind was racing, piecing together conversations I'd overheard or had with Brett: the night I'd talked to her on the phone, and Claire's reaction when she took the credit for keeping me on the show. *Was it true?*

"But it can't be true," I said. "Because I'm still here and so is Brett. She hasn't gone."

Claire nodded and glanced at the door to check if anyone was listening. Then she lowered her voice.

"Because when they told her they had no intention of firing you, she realized she couldn't win. She knew she'd never get another job after this—not at her age. So she just stayed on and carried on acting like a witch." Claire paused. "Did you really not know any of that, Ruby?"

I stared at her and shook my head. "Well, I had a few other things on my mind," I said. I couldn't believe it. I couldn't believe Brett had said all of those things about me behind my back and then had pretended that me staying was all because of her. And yet, now that Claire said it, it did all seem to fit. It seemed that I had done exactly what some of the show's viewers do. I'd mixed Brett up with Angel's mum. I was so used to being exactly like Angel that I just assumed everyone else was like their characters too.

I thanked Claire. As I walked out of the makeup room and started to make my way onto the set, my mind was racing and I felt a wave of heat sweeping across me. I felt angry, and yet, I felt free.

But it wasn't only Brett who suddenly looked like a fake. Suddenly all the house fronts and doors that led into nothing—that I used to love—looked shabby and wobbly. Even the smell seemed fake. Even I did.

If I had become so much like Angel—if Angel was really only me with a different name—then maybe I wasn't an actress at all. Maybe I was a fake too. After all, Danny made me realize that I didn't have to try to *be* her. I just *was* her. I used to be dumpy, plain Angel/Ruby and now I was still fairly dumpy, nice-hair Angel/Ruby.

I was a fraud just like Brett.

The set was already lit when I arrived; everyone was in place. I looked around and instead of seeing the moonlit garden where Angel was supposed to have her first kiss, I only saw the huge arc lights, the painted backdrop, and the hydrangea. Up until this moment, I'd really believed in this kiss: This kiss was *my* kiss. But now I saw it exactly for what it was. A fake kiss, in a wobbly set, next to a half-dead hydrangea. The kiss wouldn't be happening to *me* at all.

"Oh, Ruby, glad I caught you. Do you have a sec?" I looked up. Maria, the show's publicist, was standing at my shoulder, holding a clipboard. "I was talking to *Girls' World* magazine about you and telling them about all the letters you get and they've asked you to guest as a columnist for the magazine. What do you think? I think it would be fabulous. It would raise your profile as an actress rather than just as Angel."

"Um, yeah, whatever," I answered. One of the technicians came through the patio doors that Caspian would walk out of, and they wobbled slightly. There was a bustle by the door and Liz and Justin arrived, deep in conversation.

Liz came over and put her arm around me. "Are you ready, Ruby?" she asked me kindly.

I smiled at her. "Of course I am, Liz. It's just another scene."

She patted me on the shoulder and turned to speak to the crew. "OK, are we ready?" she shouted. "Everyone on their marks, please." I waited for my heart to skip as Justin walked over to me, but it didn't. It didn't even tremble.

"Sorry about the other day, babe," Justin whispered in my ear. "I was with my girlfriend, and I just totally forgot about it. Good old Dan the Man showed up, though, didn't he?"

I nodded silently and went to my mark by the hydrangea. I should have been heartbroken at that moment. I should have been disgusted because Justin *had* forgotten me after all. Danny had only made up all that stuff about something important coming up so I wouldn't be hurt. But I didn't feel anything. Somehow, since I found out about Brett, I'd lost the ability to feel anything about anyone. I was in shock. I suddenly knew that when Justin walked through those fake patio doors and came over to kiss me, I *would* have to act after all. I would have to act my socks off to make it look like I was in love with him. Because really and truly, I wasn't in love with him. Not me, Ruby Parker. I was just in love with the daydream version of him. To have him as a boyfriend in real life—now, *that* would be a nightmare.

"OK, take one!" somebody shouted.

"Angel?" Caspian said. "Don't stay out here on your own. Come inside—it's almost time for the cake."

"Cut!" A round of applause rippled across the set. Liz came out of the shadows and rushed up to both of us. She kissed Justin and then hugged me.

"That was wonderful, just wonderful . . . and on the first take! Perfection. You both played that just right, and as for you, Ruby . . ." Liz squeezed me again until her jewelry jangled. "Well, you were amazing. Sometimes I don't think we deserve a talent like yours. You were so convincing. You just caught Angel's feeling exactly."

Justin smiled and winked at me. "You never know, Liz," he said with a swagger. "Maybe Ruby didn't have to *act* like she was in love with me."

Everyone laughed and, as I felt my face flush bright red, I caught Danny's eye. He was standing behind one of the cameras, almost in shadow. He looked at me for a long moment, then turned around abruptly and left.

And the strangest thing was that all the butterflies and trembles and heart thumping that *didn't* happen when I kissed Justin happened just then when Danny looked at me. It was like a rock band had started a concert in my chest. I was sure anyone who looked at me right then would know the truth.

I had fallen for Danny Harvey by mistake.

"Um, Liz?" I broke into Justin and Liz's conversation. "Is it all right if I pop out for five minutes before the next scene? I need some air."

Liz patted me on the shoulder. "Off you go, Ruby. Justin and I need to sort out his motivation for the party scene anyway."

I walked off the set quickly, stopping only to pick up my bag as I went. At last I got out onto the lot. Despite its being a baking-hot day, the air still felt cool on my cheeks. I sat on the steps that go up to the auction house door that leads nowhere, pulled my phone out of my bag and called Nydia. She answered immediately.

"So how did it go?" she asked by way of a hello.

"How did what go?" I asked her. My brain was still in shock.

"Your kiss, idiot! With Justin!"

I blinked in the bright sunlight and rubbed my hand across my forehead.

"Oh, well, you know . . . it was nothing, really. We said our lines and then he kissed me. It was like he just put his lips on mine. And nothing."

There was a short silence at the other end of the line.

"Nothing?" Nydia asked, clearly disappointed.

"Nope," I told her. "Everything has turned upside down, Nydia. All of a sudden! It's like . . . I don't know. I think I've been so focused on keeping everything the same and trying to stop my life from changing that I hadn't realized I've changed too."

I looked around me. No one was there, so I could talk.

"Do you mean your highlights?" Nydia asked me seriously.

"No! I mean *me*," I told her. "Look, I haven't really got it all straight in my own head yet, but the thing is, I found out today that it was Brett who wanted me off the show . . ."

"Brett Summers!" Nydia screeched. "But she's your mentor!"

"That's what I thought," I said. "And it was a shock because I thought I could trust Brett. I thought she really did care about me. Now I realize it all was fake. And then I thought, I've been doing this for so long— I've been Angel for so long and she's been me—that

208

we've just blurred into one. Like when she had a crush on Caspian, and I had a crush on Justin. Maybe I only thought I fancied him because she did. It's like I don't know where I finish and she begins. And that's not acting. Do you know what I mean?"

"No," Nydia said, confused. I couldn't blame her; I wasn't sure *I* knew exactly what I meant.

"Well, anyway," I continued, "then today came the big scene, the all-important moment in my life—in Angel's life—and suddenly I didn't care anymore. I didn't care if I kissed Justin or a plank of wood. And, funnily enough, I don't think there would have been much difference." Nydia laughed uncertainly. "But . . . I had to *act* as if it was the most wonderful moment of my life. I had to *act* it, Nydia, and I did. And I was pretty good too." I remembered how I felt when Liz had praised me. "I got this amazing buzz from it. I can't remember the last time I had that."

"You're sure that it wasn't Justin's hot lips?" Nydia teased me.

"Yes," I told her, "because something else happened too."

"What *else* can happen to you?" Nydia exclaimed. "Don't tell me you've been abducted by aliens and are calling me from Mars."

"Even stranger," I said. "I think I fancy Danny

Harvey! I mean, I *know* I fancy Danny Harvey. It's like, he's really sweet when you get to know him. He's funny and kind and he's got this sort of slow smile and really intense eyes and I looked at him today and I got butterflies."

"Danny Harvey?" Nydia sounded confused. "I mean, I know he came to rescue you from the pizza place, but up until then he's always been grumpy, self-centered, Mr. Too-Cool-for-School Danny Harvey."

"I know!" I said. "But he's not like that at all, really, just like Anne-Marie wasn't actually evil. It makes me wonder if I really know anyone . . ."

"You know me," Nydia said glumly. "No exciting surprises here."

"Well, good," I said. "Because you're the best person in the world and I don't want that to change. Anyway, it's all pointless. I go from fancying one person who doesn't like me to fancying another person who doesn't like me in five seconds flat. How sad is that?" I watched an ant disappear into a crack in the paving and wished I could follow it.

"How do you know he doesn't fancy you?" Nydia asked blithely. "Come to think of it, he's always looking at you at school."

"He is not!" I said. "Is he? And anyway, I know

because he just gave me this look today and it was *total* loathing. So back to square one on the crush front."

"Oh, Rube," Nydia said. "Never mind, mate. At least you've still got your part in the show."

"Hmmm," I said.

"Hmmm?" Nydia said. "What does *hmmm* mean?"

"Ruby, two minutes!" one of the runners shouted at me, and I waved back.

"I've got to go, Nydia," I said. "I'll call you when I get back tonight, OK?"

We said our good-byes. Waiting just a second longer before I went back to work, I closed my eyes and turned my face into the warmth of the sun.

When I opened them, Danny was standing there! And he was smiling, which was pretty unusual for Danny. Then I realized: He must have heard me talking to Nydia!

"Oh no," I groaned. "How much did you hear?"

He sat down beside me. "Well, most of it, I think," he said with a rueful grin. "I'm sorry; it's sort of hard not to listen in when you hear your name."

I dropped my head into my hands. I knew from experience that was true.

"Oh, God," I said. "Let's just forget about it, OK? Pretend it never happened?"

Danny laughed.

"You know, you were brilliant in that scene with Justin," he said.

I forced myself to look up at him.

"Yeah?" I asked. At least he wasn't laughing outright in my face. I was right about him being sweet.

"Yeah, you really had me convinced. I thought you didn't have to act at all."

I shrugged. "I didn't think I was going to. I thought, 'Oh, no, this is my first kiss! It's got to be perfect or else my whole life is going to go wrong from this moment on.' But I was wrong. It wasn't even *my* first kiss."

Danny's brow furrowed slightly.

"No?" he asked.

"No. It was Angel's."

He smiled that sweet, slow smile again.

"Ruby, did you mean what you said before? On the phone? About liking me?"

I swallowed and bit my lip. "Well, yeah, but it's OK because I'm used to liking people who don't like me . . ."

"But I *do* like you. I really do," Danny said slowly, as if the words were hard to get out. "I've liked you since the school play. I always thought you were cool, and different from the other girls. And, well, one of the reasons I went for this part is because I thought we might get to know each other a bit better. But then it all kept going wrong and it was obvious you fancied Justin. And then when we had lunch the other day I sort of thought maybe then . . . but, well . . . I do like you, Ruby. That's what I'm trying to say."

I stared at him for a long moment before I realized that probably wasn't my most attractive look.

"Say something!" he said, laughing nervously.

"I . . . it's just that I've never had anyone like me back before. It's a bit of a shock." I made an effort to bring my eyebrows back down to the middle of my forehead.

"Ruby! Liz is waiting for you!" one of the runners hollered to me after clattering through the fire door.

"Well, I do like you. A lot," Danny said. "I think you're amazing, Ruby. And, well, I thought—I was wondering if you might, you know . . . be my girl-friend? That is, if you meant what you said."

I looked over my shoulder at the door I should have been going through right at that moment. I had never once been late to the set in all the years that I'd worked on the show—even when I'd been so into Barbies that I'd had six of them in my dressing room.

I looked back at Danny. "I'd really like that," I said. And then I think time stood still.

I couldn't hear anything and the world around us seemed to melt away. Taking my hand in his, Danny leaned in and kissed me. My heart leaped and my stomach swirled with butterflies. And it was *perfect*. My first kiss was perfect.

"Ruby?" It was Liz's voice that broke the spell. "Ruby . . . oh!" She disappeared inside quickly. Danny and I broke apart.

"I have to go," I said, grinning like a maniac.

"OK," he said. "I'll wait, shall I, until you're finished."

I almost couldn't believe this was happening to me—that this was really happening to *me* and it wasn't just a scene that someone else had scripted.

"Yes, please," I said happily. "Wait for me." And then I ran into the studio, pausing at the door to look over my shoulder. And it was then that I saw the one thing I never thought I'd *ever* see Danny Harvey do.

He was tap-dancing up the auction house steps.

Chapter Twenty

As we all filed into the hall for the first assembly of the new school year, I looked over my shoulder and caught Danny's eye. He winked at me and smiled and my tummy did a little jump. Danny Harvey was a great boyfriend—a funny, kind, and sweet boyfriend who I could actually talk to. Even Nydia thought so after we all went bowling together: her, me, Anne-Marie, and Michael Henderson. (She never did chuck him.) The rest of the summer break went so quickly after that first kiss with Danny—too quickly.

When we got back to school, I thought there'd be dramas about me and Danny, and about Anne-Marie suddenly becoming friends with Nydia and me. But there hasn't been. After Nydia and I spent hours and hours practicing our catty comebacks and writing them down in a notebook so we wouldn't forget them like we always used to (Nydia's idea), we didn't need any of them at all. It wasn't as if Jade and Menakshi and the gang suddenly wanted to hang out with us and paint our nails, but they didn't make nasty comments about us every time we saw them or write stuff about us in their notebooks. All those months of feeling isolated and peculiar just vanished as if they'd never happened in the first place. And it seemed to me that everyone was rather glad about that—almost relieved. I mean, it takes up a lot of energy being so nasty. It might have been because they saw the light and realized what great girls Nydia and I are. It might have been because Anne-Marie flits between their group and ours, gradually drawing us all closer together.

Or it could be because I left the show at the end of the season and I will never go back (although Liz says she will always keep a door open for me anyway), so I haven't been going on about my job all the time.

Dad was fine with my decision. He was the first person I told (after Nydia and then Danny—oh, and Anne-Marie) because I knew how Mum would react and I wanted to talk it over with him first. When I went round to his flat, I felt a bit guilty, like I was

216

going behind her back. But then I realized that if he had still been living at home, I would have talked to him first anyway. He was still my dad. I was still allowed to confide in him.

He'd handed me a glass of fresh-squeezed orange juice and listened to me as I explained why I wanted to leave.

"It's just that I think I need a change, Dad—a challenge. I think I need to go through what everyone else at school is doing—going up for auditions, even if I don't get them, experiencing different things, and learning more. I've been on the show so long, I'm almost stuck there."

Dad furrowed his brow.

"Well, I agree with you, Ruby. But are you sure this is your idea and not this *Danny's*?" He said Danny's name cautiously, and I smiled to myself. I knew Mum would be fine about Danny and terrible about me leaving *Kensington Heights*, and I knew that Dad would be exactly the opposite.

"Yes, it's my idea," I told him firmly. "It's what *I* want."

Dad nodded. "You know, some people leave soaps and are never heard of again by the public. That could be you—you understand that?"

I nodded. "Yes, Dad. But it's better to take the

chance, don't you think? It was more or less luck that got me the job on the show, and I was too young to even know it. I want it to be *talent* that gets me my next job."

He smiled at me. "I'm happy for you, Ruby, I really am. You make me very proud." He gave me a little hug and then coughed and looked a bit embarrassed.

"Now, about this Danny . . ."

"Oh, Dad." I rolled my eyes. "I'm thirteen, not completely mental, OK? I'm not going to jump into bed with him, I'm not going to elope with him, I'm not going to smoke or do drugs or rob a bank with him, OK? He's just a really nice boy and I like him. We have fun."

My dad looked like he was about to say something and then he closed his mouth.

"OK," he said reluctantly. "Bring him round sometime."

"I will," I said.

Mum tried to talk me out of it.

"But, Ruby, you are the luckiest girl in the world! Do you know how lucky you are? Millions of girls would *kill* to do what you're doing; all the girls in your school would."

I thought of Anne-Marie secretly hating me for

being so smug about *Kensington Heights*.

"How many times do you think you've asked me that, Mum? I think I know how lucky I am," I said. "But . . . I need a change." Then I told her all the things I told Dad, but she didn't seem to see.

"But you're secure there," she insisted. "You don't have to worry about getting rejected, and Liz said she'd do anything to keep you on."

I shrugged again and looked at Everest. He winked at me (or possibly at my sandwich). "I know, but . . ." A thought crossed my mind. "Do we need the money?" I asked her. "For us, and the school fees, I mean?"

Mum shook her head quickly and sat down at the table. "No, no, love. It's not that. There's enough for you to stay there until you've done your exams. It's not the money. It's *you* I'm worried about. You have what most actors dream of—steady work. Out there in the big world there's rejection after rejection. It's tough, Ruby, and it hurts. Do you really want that? And why now?"

I looked into her eyes.

"I don't know." I thought for a moment. "No, I *do* know. I used to want things to always be the same, and I couldn't wait to be grown up and be in control of my own life. But now everything's changed and I realize it's going to be OK. Maybe even better. I know you and Dad aren't together and it's hard and sad and different, but I also know that we're going to be fine. I want to make some of my own changes. This is what I want. And besides . . ." I left the bit I knew she'd like the best till last. "I want to put school first for a while anyway." I smiled at her. "And if I do get knocked back, I'll just keep on going. That's the thing about dreams, isn't it, Mum? You have to follow them, right?"

Mum smiled and picked up my hand.

"Ruby Parker," she said, "you are an amazing girl."

And that was it, I thought as I settled down to listen to Sylvia Lighthouse lecture us for the millionth time on dedication and determination. All the ups and downs, all the roller-coaster rides of the last few weeks were gradually flattening out. Things were going to be nice and quiet and just normal for the foreseeable future. Ruby Parker hits the small time.

"Students." The buzzing in the hall died as Sylvia Lighthouse began to speak. "I have an announcement to make. Usually I would do this sort of thing in private, but on this occasion I think it merits an announcement."

Sylvia Lighthouse looked around the hall with her gimlet eyes. I wondered if she was going to expel someone. You could never tell until the last minute if she was pleased or cross with you.

"Yesterday I spoke with a Mr. Art Dubrovnik . . ." A murmur swept around the hall. I turned to Nydia, my eyes wide. "As you may know, Mr. Dubrovnik is one of Hollywood's leading directors, with two Academy Awards under his belt." Nydia and I exchanged impressed looks. "Later on this year he will commence directing his latest film to be set in London. It will star Imogen Grant."

Nydia's eyes widened. "Imogen Grant! A real, proper movie star!" she whispered along with everyone else in the hall.

"Quiet, please!" Sylvia Lighthouse's tone stopped the murmur dead.

"Mr. Dubrovnik wishes to cast a young girl between the ages of twelve and fourteen to play alongside Ms. Grant in the film. I'm afraid I don't know very much about the part yet, but all will be revealed, I'm sure. Now, there will not be open auditions as there is limited time, so Mr. Dubrovnik has asked me to pick six girls from this school to screen-test for him. There will also be twelve more girls from other . . . sources." Sylvia Lighthouse wrinkled her nose with distaste at the thought of other stage schools. "It was a hard choice—you are all very talented—so please don't be disappointed if you're not on the list." She coughed and all the girls in the school between twelve and fourteen sat on the edge of their seats.

"Scarlett James."

One of the girls in the year below us screamed.

"Silence, please!" Sylvia Lighthouse bellowed. "Any further commotion and *none* of you will be going. Do you understand?"

The whole school held its breath.

"Now, the remaining five: Anne-Marie Chance, Nydia Assimin, Selena Rivers, Olivia Green, and Ruby Parker."

Silence echoed throughout the hall.

"Will those six girls please come and see me in my study at break?" Sylvia looked at all of us. "You may applaud."

Anne-Marie and Nydia and I flung our arms around each other and screamed.

"Me! She picked me!" Nydia said. "I've been picked! Something has happened to me!"

"It's amazing. All three of us!" I said, laughing. "It's a miracle!"

"I know—and not because of my dad, either!" Anne-Marie laughed.

"We'll be up against each other, though," I said as we walked out of the hall with our arms around each other. "Only one person will get it. It might not even be one of us."

Nydia linked her arm though mine and then Anne-Marie's. "I know," she said. "But we get to try, don't we? We get to try!"

"And whoever gets it, we'll all be happy, right?" Anne-Marie asked. Nydia and I nodded. "Even if it's none of us."

The bell rang for first period and Danny ran up behind us and took my hand, drawing me a couple of paces back from the others.

"So, next stop Hollywood, hey, Rube?" he said with a grin.

"Who knows?" I said, smiling at him. "And to think I was going to have a quiet life."

our best issue ever!

teen girl! magazine

Inside:

Exclusive interview with
ex–Kensington Heights
star Ruby Parker. . .

 pop gossip! cute new looks! top tips!

teen girl!

Magazine's 60-Second Interview

talks exclusively to TV's most popular teen actress, Ruby Parker, now that she has left hit show *Kensington Heights*.

tg: Ruby, you've recently announced that you've left *Kensington Heights*. What's in store for you next?

rp: Well, I'm not really sure yet, and that's what's so exciting. I mean, I know I've got a lot of hard work to do at school—that never changes. But as for my next acting job? Well, like you, I'll hve to wait and see.

tg: Any big auditions coming up?

rp: (Laughs) Maybe. I can't really say anything at this stage.

tg: So, what TG readers really want to know is—are the rumors true about you and fellow *Kensington Heights* actor Danny Harvey? Is he your boyfriend? He's gorgeous!

rp: (Laughs again) Danny and I worked together on *Kensington Heights* and we go to the same school. So yes, we are very good friends, and that's all I'm saying!

tg: OK. Look, thousands of our readers would love a career in acting and TV, and they want to be just like you. What advice would you give to all of those girls?

rp: I'd say to follow your dream, if that's what you really want. It takes a lot of hard work and determination. There are ups and downs, rejections as well as successes. But if you work hard and have talent, there's no reason—no reason at all— why you couldn't be just like me.